Mothering a Muslim

Mothering a Muslim

Nazia Erum

juggernaut

JUGGERNAUT BOOKS
KS House, 118 Shahpur Jat, New Delhi 110049, India

First published in hardback by Juggernaut Books 2017
Published in paperback 2018

Most names have been changed to protect the identity of the students

10 9 8 7 6 5 4 3 2

ISBN 9788193876718

Typeset in Adobe Caslon Pro by R. Ajith Kumar, Noida

Printed at Thomson Press India Ltd

For Myra, where it all began
Yasser, who makes it all possible
& Nana Abbu, who predicted it all

Contents

I am invisible, simply because people refuse to see me

– *Invisible Man*, Ralph Ellison

Author's note

Our earliest memories shape us as people. We might add a new layer of learnings on a foundation of grainy ideals, but at our core we hold on to the beliefs and ideas we absorbed as children. The ones our mother taught us. Mothers are our bridges between the inner and outer worlds. I believe they are our first shelter and our last refuge.

When I became a mother myself I immediately felt the weight of the task ahead. The year was 2014. And our country stood divided along religious fault lines. Within the minority Muslim population, a fear was palpable. As I held my little daughter, Myra, for the first time, the fear found a place in me too. I was worried of even giving her a Muslim-sounding name. But as an educated, working metropolitan woman, I wanted to reject this unnamed fear. I wanted to work towards a bright, positive future for my daughter. I wondered if that was possible.

As I tuned in to the conversations around me, I found little that looked at the Muslim motherhood experience from an urban middle-class perspective. I wanted to know whether a Muslim mother's worries were any different from that of her Hindu, Christian or Sikh counterparts. What were the challenges that were exclusively hers? And why had I never heard of them before? What did it mean to raise Muslim children today in this increasingly polarized world? So I set forth on a journey to fill this empty narrative space, believing we are in parts every woman we meet in life.

This book is that journey.

I was unprepared for what lay ahead. The stories that tumbled out of closets were unbelievable and often devastating. I reached out to 145 families across twelve cities over a span of a year for my research. To begin with, I was clear I did not want to speak with women living in all-Muslim neighbourhoods. I wanted families, like mine, who have always lived in mixed localities and prefer to do so. Families that actively live the idea of India in their day-to-day lives.

Next I wanted to document the lived experiences of the urban, educated Muslim women and their families. The 'authentic Muslim woman' is so much more than a symbol – but she is mostly missing in our media-driven discourse.

During the course of my research, I met many 'authentic Muslim women'. There was a feisty hijabi principal; a burkha-clad single mother of two who was an ex-Facebook and ex-Google employee; an Urdu- and paan-loving 'patriarch'; a bob-haired child psychologist; a gynaecologist in a niqab; a district-level swimmer; a state-level basketball player; a dentist; an advocate; an IT professional; and a shayara. A homemaker; a university lecturer; a civil rights advocate; and a development professional. A member of Parliament; an author; an activist; and a feminist.

My 'authentic Muslim woman' drives in her veil, she puts a bindi on her face. She is your neighbour, your child's schoolteacher. She is everywhere if you care to look.

They were a varied bunch but most of them told a single story – that they were worried and fearful for their children, many of whom were targets of Islamophobia and nationalism in their classrooms and playgrounds. I was shaken by their stories. I was advised not to publish my findings, lest I become a target of bigotry.

But the large-scale incidence and the under-reporting of the subject worried me immensely. Eighty-five per cent of the hundred-plus children I spoke to told me that they had been bullied, hit or ostracized at school because of their religion. Even after I had completed my research for this book, I kept hearing more and more such stories from all across the country. And yet we don't speak of it openly even within the Muslim community. The malaise is growing but not too many people know about it as the victims' parents talk only to their circle of friends and family – and rarely to the school and media. The problem is compounded by the fact that the urban middle-class Muslim is intimidated by her own largely conservative community.

I worried for the children facing the communal bullying all alone at school without anyone recognizing or willing to acknowledge their plight.

I worried for my daughter who will be joining them tomorrow in the same playgrounds and classrooms. We need to speak, not for ourselves, but for our children.

I have mentioned the names of the schools where children have been targeted for being Muslim in order to ground the book, and make my readers see that Islamophobia cuts across class and economics. But this is not so much a reflection of the classrooms as of the society we have become. The names are only to add nuance to our understanding of the world we have created for our children. Make no mistake, these schools are not where the problem begins or ends. Nor are they alone facing this. I fear it might be a problem in every school, at every level of our society.

Nor are the schools to blame. In most instances the school administration is not even aware of this problem because the children or their parents rarely complain to the authorities. While some schools remained indifferent when complaints were registered, some others made efforts to sensitize their students to accepting and embracing the 'other'. Only some schools have been named within the chapters, in cases where the identity of the student was not being compromised. I have included at the end of the book a full list of the schools where my subjects study or studied. I have also noted in which schools the incidents were brought to the attention of the teachers and in which cases they were not reported.

The situation is complex and I sincerely hope all schools will take this as an eye-opener and individually and collectively think of measures to counter the hate that seems to be in the air.

Otherwise we will be guilty of setting these young people on the path to becoming hate-filled adults. Today's high school pass-outs will be voting in the next national elections in 2019 and today's class 5 students will be eligible to vote in the 2024 elections. Hate affects not just the tormented but also the tormentor.

This is not just a lone mother's fight. This is a fight for all of us.

1

The Muslims are coming

Her terrified scream echoed shrilly in the closed space of the car. They were everywhere, the mass of white-clad bodies. They had surrounded the car from all sides. Most of the faces had long beards and black marks on their foreheads. She had spent many nights imagining the horns that grew on that spot. They had finally found her too.

She felt panic grip her heart, squeezing it tight. Her skin broke into goosebumps. Her short hair was sticky with sweat. She ducked under the back seat of the car, and uttered the words that were choking her throat. 'The Muslims are coming... They will kill us!'

Arshia Shah and Harris Alvi turned around in surprise to look at their five-year-old daughter, Azania. They couldn't hold back their laughter.

Azania had just started school in a posh South Delhi locality. She knew she was an Indian, but not that she was a Muslim. She knew of Allah. But not that only Muslims believed in Allah. What is a good age to tell a child that she belongs to a particular religion? When does a child begin to associate the sound of a name with a particular religion? These were not questions Arshia and Harris had asked of themselves.

The couple had set out on an extended weekend break to Aligarh with their little girl for the annual visit to the grandparents. Their route took in many small towns that dotted western Uttar Pradesh. It was noon, and the Friday jamaat, prayer congregation, was dispersing from a masjid in one such small town. The road was crowded with cars and worshippers who were heading back home. Clad in pearly white kurta-pyjama and skullcaps, they walked and talked happily, with the words of the khutbah, the Friday sermon, still on their minds. Little did they know that inside a hatchback on that road a terrified five-year-old was cowering under the back seat as she screamed again to emphasize the urgency, 'The Muslims are coming!'

Azania's parents' first reaction had been amusement at the irony of a Muslim child cowering in fear of Muslims. They comforted her and told her there was nothing to fear. They urged her to look out of the window and see for herself that none of the men on the road were carrying weapons or seemed angry or had even noticed her. Azania calmed down. Her parents giggled. But underneath the laughter lurked some serious questions. A silence permeated the car for the rest of the trip.

Arshia had no idea from where Azania had picked up the word Muslim and the stereotypes associated with it. Could it be at her playgroup or nursery school? The little girl had clearly internalized that Muslims were violent. How do you tell a five-year-old that she is what she fears?

A buoyant group outside on the road. A bewildered child inside the car. And a set of parents unable to figure out where to start talking about the elephant in the room: Islam.

Not quite knowing how to deal with this, Arshia didn't talk to Azania during that trip. She wanted to find the right moment for both herself and her daughter. But she didn't have to wait. Azania found out the truth about herself soon after.

2

The elephant in the schools

'Get away from the ball, you Paki!'

Azania stopped just as she was about to kick the blue-yellow ball with her white canvas shoes and turned indignantly towards the boy from the rival football team. As she stood still in shock, not knowing how to react, he tackled the ball off her.

The little girl slipped fearfully out of the football field of her school, Vasant Valley. The boy was known to be aggressive and competitive. But why had he called her a Paki? She felt confused and didn't know who to talk to and chose to remain silent.

~

Azania Safiya Khan had the distinction of being the only one in her family who had 'Khan' as her surname. Arshia Shah tells me that her daughter was named Azania – an ancient Hebrew name – by her maternal grandmother. Arshia had instantly loved it. Azania's middle name is Safiya, which was shared by feisty great-grandmothers on both sides of the family.

Arshia had decided to keep her surname after her marriage. 'I did not want Azania to get only her dad's last name as I feel that she is equally my child. At the same time, I do not like hyphenated names. So her last name had to be something which came from both her father and her mother (like her middle name did). So we decided to revive the name Khan which both my husband's family and mine had dropped over the years for being too common a last name.

'So although my husband and I are not immediately identifiable as Muslims by our names, our daughter is clearly tagged as a Muslim because of the surname Khan. We did not realize this at the time of naming her, just like our parents were not consciously thinking about whether our names sound Muslim or not, when they named us. They gave us names which sounded nice to them.'

Many factors come into play when we look for the perfect name – its meaning, the way it sounds, the things we associate with it. But increasingly for Muslims there is another factor – the weight of social acceptance. I remember feeling a kind of fear when I first held my tiny newborn, wrapped in creamy soft chenille, in my arms. I had looked into her velvety, crumpled face and wondered what the right name for her would be. Should I choose a name that signalled her religion, like Fatima, or pick a modern and neutral-sounding name, like Myra, to avoid too much spotlight on her being Muslim. I settled for the latter.

It was in these early days that I began to seek out other Muslim mothers who were in the same boat as me. How deep was the concern over our identities? I found that many new Muslim parents today choose the middle ground, preferring not to go for an overtly Islamic name. This is all right if it's a choice. But increasingly it's a need. Why, you ask. Read on.

~

Bewildered, Azania Safiya Khan did not tell her parents of her day at the football field. It was only many months later, when she had safely distanced herself from the disturbing memory, that she hesitantly asked her mother about it. A stunned Arshia found herself completely unprepared for this. She was a highly educated woman with a bright corporate career who had never publicly expressed her Muslim identity. She believed in giving her daughter a liberal upbringing and had never factored in her Muslim-ness being thrust upon her daughter. But now it was.

Arshia sat down with Azania and spoke to her. She recounts, 'I told her that if anyone else ever said this again, she must ask them what they meant and why they were saying it. She must make it a point to correct them and not quietly accept it. Also [she should] try not to go about tattling, because sometimes the person you tattle to also may not be able to do anything about it. But you have to learn how to put a stop to such talk without taking help from anyone else. I decided not to take any action myself because firstly some time had passed and secondly because to some extent I could understand, although not justify, where that offensive and insensitive statement came from. The boy was a Kashmiri Pandit. I always regret how the Muslim community never came out strongly enough to condemn the exodus of KPs or the '84 riots. We just did not do enough.'

But little Azania could not decipher the connection between the boy's antecedents and his unwarranted taunt. After all she was only a third grader. 'It was hard to explain this to Azania. I just told her that it was wrong of the boy to say that. I certainly made it a point to speak more positively about Islam and Muslims after these incidents and separate terrorism from Islam. But later the more I thought about it, I felt I wasn't doing enough.'

Was this an isolated incident? Had such prejudice always existed? I remember my elder brother once being referred to as 'Hamas' – the terrorist outfit that was a household name in our pre-9/11 world of the 1990s – when he went to school wrapped up in his winter muffler. Back then such a quip was both rare and light-hearted, the smiles and giggles accompanying the banter between friends on a cold foggy morning signifying the absence of any hatred or fear. We too didn't make a big deal of it, though it pinched and stayed with us.

I asked an older cousin, Shehla Rafat. She didn't have a similar experience in the 1980s, but her younger sister, who now teaches at the prestigious St Stephen's College, was called a terrorist when she was studying in a South Delhi school in the 1990s. The pattern repeated recently when Shehla's eight-year-old son Aatish joined the Shiv Nadar School in Noida, established by a leading global enterprise. From his story and Azania's, it was clear that these experiences were not a joke to be dismissed. The banter I remembered as a young girl had gathered weight, from years of angry news headlines and television debates. Today they are hurled like stones.

But was I picking up isolated incidents? After all, no one discussed this in the so-called liberal middle-class circles I inhabited. I began to ask more and more Muslim parents of young and adolescent children: 'Has your child been called a terrorist or a Pakistani in school?' Initially it seemed that I was paranoid. A cousin in Faridabad was appalled. 'No way. Things aren't that bad yet.' A close friend in Friends Colony said, 'Nopes, never heard. Are you crazy?'

Then I asked a friend who worked with a group of young Muslim girls. 'Of course, being called a Pakistani is like a long-running joke. Just like

Sardar jokes!' I checked with my neighbour, Arifa Beig. Both her boys, aged sixteen and twelve, had also been called a Pakistani or a terrorist. And the incidents weren't stray ones. 'It's so common,' she said with a sigh.

I made a list of the leading schools in Delhi and began calling up everyone I knew with young kids for referrals to Muslim parents. I asked journalists, I asked teachers, I asked doctors, I asked lawyers, I asked chartered accountants, I asked and I asked.

I ended up interviewing 118 Muslim families with children between five and twenty years of age who were studying or had studied in twenty-two leading schools across South Delhi, Gurugram (formerly Gurgaon) and Noida. Of these a hundred students said they had been called a terrorist or a Pakistani at some point in school by a classmate.

The figures were alarming. I looked for the stories behind the numbers.

~

My neighbour Arifa, a forty-five-year-old art curator, is the mother of two boys, who studied in the Lotus Valley International School on the Noida–Greater Noida expressway. A major terrorist attack had occurred the night before. Saad, her ten-year-old younger son, was then in class 5. In his classroom, the newspaper was lying on the teacher's desk as the students waited for their English class to start. The teacher walked in, picked up the newspaper and read aloud the headlines about the attack to the class. 'What is happening in the world!' she exclaimed with a sigh as she sat down. Suddenly, one of the students called out Saad's name loudly. '*Saaad, yeh kya kar diya tumne?* [What did you do, Saaad?]'

There was silence in the class. The words stuck in Saad's throat. He felt all eyes on him, waiting for him to say something. He was hot and angry. But he couldn't find the words to retaliate. The question settled uncomfortably in the classroom, filling the air with tension. Through the incident, the teacher did not bother to look up. 'I kept waiting for my teacher to react and scold the classmate, but she didn't react. She kept sitting there in front of us without saying a word. After a while she stood up and began the class. I was silent, I didn't respond and kept sitting there. I didn't really know what to do.'

Arifa says the unmistakable changes came in after the national election campaigns in 2014. 'People just became very in-your-face with their feelings about Muslims. And this I noticed was being reflected in their children at school. Bullying had always existed, but it was different before, largely comprising childish rebukes and stupid, dumb things being said to each other in schools. This has changed now. When a Muslim student is bullied it is on pronounced religious lines. Now he is called Baghdadi, Bangladeshi, Pakistani or simply a terrorist. Everyone's speech is borrowed from the language used in the news [channels].'

While such slurs have been used since the 1990s, the tone and intensity have changed, especially over the last five years. Earlier the remarks were innocuous and infrequent. Now they occur more often and are marked by hostility rather than humour. Not that humour justifies the taunts. It shows how deeply entrenched the association of a Muslim to terror is. The context is different now and possibly feeds on the changes – global terrorism in the name of Islam has increased dramatically over the last fifteen years with ISIL (or ISIS) alone responsible for 95 per cent of deaths from claimed terrorist attacks.[1]

At the same time, the past decade has seen a rise in Hindu right-wing sentiment within India and a slew of distorted narratives that portray Muslims as invaders, anti-national and a threat to national security. These took centre stage in the run-up to the polarizing national elections of 2014. From my conversations with many others across the country, it seems this consciousness has now been handed down to the children of our country.

Arifa's elder son, Raffat, was called a 'terrorist' casually in a fight when he was seventeen years old in 2016. Arifa was appalled and immediately contacted the mother of the name-caller through the class WhatsApp group. 'But your kid also called my child names! He called him *fat*!' was all that the mother had to say.

'She was actually defending her boy and

---

[1] The Global Terrorism Index 2015, p. 20. http://economicsandpeace.org/wp-content/uploads/2015/11/Global-Terrorism-Index-2015.pdf

equating a terrorist to fat. I had nothing more to say to her. The kids had been friends from a long time,' recounts Arifa, shaking her head. She took the matter to the class teacher. 'There was no action. They simply said that they would talk to the parents. But then it kept happening repeatedly. And after a while my boys refused to report it to the school authorities,' Arifa said.

As the brothers have grown older, they have become pricklier. Even though they still get bullied, they don't want to appear like sissies and carry tales to their mother, preferring to 'fight it out'. The verbal abuses often turn into physical scuffles and fights in the playground or school buses. Arifa is usually very vocal and assertive of her rights, but in this case, over time she has given in to silence. 'I keep asking them to not react as the political climate is such. One never knows when things get blown out of proportion,' says Arifa sadly, with a tinge of fear in her voice.

Raffat disagrees. 'If they think we are terrorists then we will show them what we can do. How can they say that to us? Every time there is a terror attack in the news, my classmates ask me the next day, *Arre yeh kya karwa diya tumne?* [What have you done now?] As if I am responsible!' When I asked Raffat why he gets into physical fights instead of complaining to the school authorities, he says that there is no point in trying to reason away the unreasonable. 'If they want to fight, we cannot shy away!' said the visibly upset young man.

The bullies are only repeating what they hear in their homes. Our conversations are laced with hate and awareness of the 'other', and it is natural for children to start mirroring this in their words. Arifa says, 'I told my boys it's best to ignore such absurd comments. Because they all have to together travel in buses and study. It's not possible to avoid each other or live in animosity. It could lead to being pushed out from groups or being cold-shouldered.'

Arifa's comment reminded me of eleven-year-old Maaz, who studies in class 6 in a branch of Delhi Public School in the national capital region (NCR). Born to parents in an inter-religious marriage, he tells me how he is socially boycotted by his classmates due to his Muslim surname. He is often called a terrorist and nobody wants to play with him. 'They are all busy playing with each other and don't include me,' he tells me forlornly. 'I sit with a Muslim girl during the tiffin break. She has some friends who are OK with me. I have no friends,' says Maaz.

Quite often, the battles start even earlier. 'My little one is only six and a half years old and got hit for being a Muslim in school,' says Zareen Siddique, whose daughter Samaira studies in an internationally accredited school in Noida. A student sitting on the same bench as her asked, 'Are you a Muslim?' He then started hitting Samaira, saying 'I hate Muslims.' Zareen says it took a few days before her daughter could open up about it. 'I was appalled and shocked. I immediately called up the class teacher who had a two-word response, "It happens."'

However, the teacher did try to find a resolution and informed the parents of the child. But they said, 'You are lying. My kid isn't like that.' The teacher, a Muslim herself, told Zareen, 'There is a lot of denial but you can't help it, the children carry the biases of their parents to the classrooms. It's from both the sides, both Muslims and Hindus. So often during a class educational tour, the Muslim children will refuse to enter a mandir.

Or the Hindu children will refuse to stand with the Muslims. There is only so much we can do to sensitize the kids. How can we tell them that their parents are wrong?'

Zareen says, 'I have noticed these changes in the last few years. My elder kid has been in the same school for the past seven years but never faced anything like this. Only in the past two years do these incidents seem to be arising. But six- or seven-year-olds are just too young for such hate.'

There seems to be a growing tension that is going unchecked. Zareen asks me how long she can ask her kids to ignore this. I have no answer for her. She says, 'It will affect them. I think we should move out of India.' I tell her to hold on.

~

The students I spoke to were mostly from expensive, upper-middle-class schools. If targeting Muslims was so rampant in the elite sections, I wondered what a similar survey in other social sections might throw up. I also saw patterns emerging from the interviews. Incidents of religious bullying get reported much more in junior classes but are dismissed as stray or juvenile cases. In higher classes like 7–12 the attacks are more vicious, but go largely under-reported. It often borders on violence among boys but is mostly in the form of subtle jokes among girls. For example, '*Kya tumhare mamma papa bomb banate hain?* [Do your parents make bombs at home?]' or 'Don't piss her off, she will bomb you!'

As Azania Safiya Khan grew up, she never again faced physical aggression but in recent years in senior secondary she often faced jokes targeted at her and her religion. Her classmates would say, 'Is your father part of the Taliban? Will he shoot all of us?' or ones laced with misogyny along with Islamophobia like 'Isn't your father angry that your legs are exposed in your skirt? Not that your legs are very shapely!' Her mother, Arshia, says, 'All this was said in jest. It was supposed to be funny. Other kids would laugh and Azania was expected to laugh as well. Her not laughing was seen as oversensitivity or not having a sense of humour.'

Most Muslim children, even when they have not faced any direct aggressive communal bullying, will definitely identify with such low-key but repetitive comments. Such jokes usually don't ring alarm bells for parents. Many mothers dismissed such incidents as harmless banter that need not be given undue importance. While physical violence is immediately recognized as damaging, verbal violence is seldom recognized for the harm it can cause. Verbal violence can be not only offensive, but harmful as the implied meanings are internalized by our young. Research says that a culture of constant, casual brutality and simmering stress is toxic to the body.

Lisa Feldman Barrett, professor of psychology at Northeastern University in the United States and author of *How Emotions Are Made: The Secret Life of the Brain*, says, 'By all means, we should have open conversations and vigorous debate about controversial or offensive topics. But we must also halt speech that bullies and torments. From the perspective of our brain cells, the latter is literally a form of violence.'[2] This is especially the case among girls, who are restrained by the social conditioning of silence from 'giving it back' with violence. I asked the mothers if Muslim kids can retaliate

[2] https://www.nytimes.com/2017/07/14/opinion/sunday/when-is-speech-violence.html

in the same way – can a non-Muslim student be called a terrorist or Pakistani in 'harmless jokes'? The answer was almost always a vehement no.

From the 1990s onward those raising a child have had to grapple with the impact of terrorism, demonizing of Muslims and the lack of a fact-based, age-appropriate discussion to process this has had on young impressionable and vulnerable minds. The grandparents of today's Muslim youth would themselves have been children during Partition or may have been born after Independence. Partition stories are fables for them, they come from a faraway time. They only know of their motherland, India, and they are proud Indians. How do they get their head around being called a Pakistani? Or worse, a terrorist. And in what ways will these trails of prejudice follow them in the future as they grow up and try to make a life for themselves in their homeland? It is a troubling reality that we are bequeathing to the younger generation.

Shehla Rafat says, 'There is a lot of anger in the kid. He/She wonders, how can my friend call me such names? So part of the counselling I did for my kid was that it's all right to be a Pakistani. And the other part was that you are not a Pakistani. So your friend was wrong.' Mostly young kids don't know what a Pakistani or a terrorist means but they can internalize a negative meaning from the tone when they are bullied. This intonation can also affect their sense of religion and self-worth.

Shehla narrated one of the most positive responses I heard in the course of my research for this book. The Shiv Nadar School where her son studied reacted splendidly when she brought up the incident with them. They took the opportunity to sensitively introduce the students to concepts of 'us vs them' in different contexts over a week-long session. It was not made out to be only about the two boys but about all the various differences that make up India – caste, region, language, etc., with religion being only one of the differences. My research did not throw up any other examples of such prompt and well-thought-out school action. That is probably because such incidents largely go unreported. Most children and parents are embarrassed about it and believe they are stray incidents. But the less they talk and report about it, the more it keeps happening.

Asiya Shervani, who has rich experience in the

education sector consulting on gender and social inclusion, says, 'We cannot hold only schools and teachers accountable. Teachers are a part of the larger society which is becoming increasingly intolerant, vocally and openly. Training expert teachers requires huge investment of time, effort and support and its success depends on a nurturing policy environment. Even the best of schools invest mostly in teachers' knowledge and assessment skills. What goes for a toss is how the teachers can help students build healthy identities. If we can't handle discussing sex or sexual abuse, then how will we handle cases of misogyny, homophobia, casteism and, in the last decade or so, the rise of Islamophobia, which has certainly moved from our drawing rooms to the classrooms and school corridors. Students who are victimized are rarely going to report the matter to their teachers.'

Asiya says most bullying cases go unreported and more so when these have religious associations. Children learn to cope with them in their own way. Leave alone teachers, children often don't even tell their parents. Even when they do, how will Muslim parents have the courage to report bullying of their child on the basis of religion, in a school where there are hardly any Muslim teachers or students? However, if schools highlight at the beginning of each year that they believe in equality and respect and that they mean it and are alert about it, it may be easier for students and parents to speak out.

Asiya adds that children will only confide in their teachers or even their parents, for that matter, about their complex problems if they are sure that these adults can handle them without making things worse for them. 'I don't think our kids trust us yet. The key question is, how do we make ourselves worthy of their trust? Anti-Muslim sentiment cannot be tackled without tackling all the other prejudices we have based on otherization. I refuse to talk about Islamophobia without talking about all other kinds of discrimination. I see a linkage all the way. However, as educationists we have to also be aware of the compounded nature of hatred towards Muslims. Islamophobia permeates all forms of discrimination.'

~

The Sanskriti School in Delhi's Diplomatic Enclave was founded primarily to provide education to children of bureaucrats and the defence forces. It has been consistently among the top-ranked schools in the city. Here, Saira Alam was admitted into class 8 when her parents got transferred to Delhi.

In her first year at the school, Saira experienced a lot of gender-based bullying from boys. They would grab her school bag and take it to the boys' washroom and explore its contents. 'There was a whole lot of slut shaming by showing off her sanitary napkins and they would call her a whore. And these were all boys from the best of families,' says Saira's mother. But the bullying changed in nature after 2013 as the national election campaigns started all over India. Some of the students were verbally violent to her and many times she was told to 'go to Pakistan'.

'She refused to let me complain to the school authorities as she said few of her friends supported her and she would handle it on her own. But I was very worried. This was the first time Saira became aware of her identity as a Muslim. These incidents were unacceptable to us. We are from the defence forces ourselves. We have given, and continue to give, a lot of sweat, blood and hard work to uphold the integrity of this nation. No one can take that away from us. No one can take away our pride at being Indians.'

A few months later when Saira was excluded from the Interact Club at school, she asked her mother, 'Is it because I am a Muslim?' Saira at a young age had internalized being a victim.

~

Such stories are rampant in Delhi, but there are echoes of this all over India. For example, religious bullying is on the rise in boarding schools across India, from Nainital to Bengaluru. Alpana, a banker, was shocked when her son who had just come back from his first semester at boarding school in Bengaluru asked her, 'Can we make friends with Muslims? Should they all go to Pakistan?' The confusion had arisen because the house master had separated the eight Muslim boys in his batch, putting four in one dorm and the other four in another dorm saying that if they were all put together in one dorm they would make a 'Pakistan' of the hostel dorms.

I heard of only a few cases in Lucknow,

Hyderabad, Bengaluru and Pune, but they are prevalent. Mumbai has had an awareness of religious differences in young children since a long time but it has bordered around bias over food preferences and carrying non-vegetarian food in tiffins. On the whole, it has not yet become as widespread as in Delhi–NCR.

But with the rabid reinforcement of the Hindutva agenda across the country, and redrawing of religious fault lines, it is not hard to imagine this soon becoming a nationwide phenomenon. This is not just happening in India but in many places around the world, most visibly in the United States after its 2016 presidential campaign. Leading publications in the West have reported on the effect of 'Trump Talk' on America's schools.[3] A report by the Teacher Tolerance Project in April 2016 says, 'Teachers have noted an increase in bullying, harassment and intimidation of students whose races, religions or nationalities have been the verbal targets of candidates on the campaign

[3] https://www.washingtonpost.com/news/answer-sheet/wp/2016/11/06/the-frightening-effect-of-trump-talk-on-americas-schools/?utm_term=.bd5f44ea4a25

trail.' The report states that over 90 per cent of educators said the school climate had been negatively affected by the elections with children imitating political rhetoric in word, tone and behaviour.

We don't know yet what the far-reaching implications of this will be on the lives of our children. They are growing up in a society that has normalized hostility and hate. Sayyara Ansari, senior psychologist, Columbia-Asia group of hospitals, Gurugram-Delhi, says, 'This will be a confused generation uncomfortable with identities. They will become either very aggressive or very withdrawn. They won't go the middle course.'

Let us travel to an upscale 'posh' boarding school in Indore for our next story where the question remains the same: How do you explain such attacks to a kid under ten years or as young as six?

How can you say 'he is only a child' to another child?

Six-year-old Rohit [*curiously, out of the blue*]: *Kya tum Mussulman ho?* [Are you a Muslim?] *Your name sounds so.*

Six-year-old Amir [*seriously*]: *Yes, I am a Muslim. Main non-veg khata hoon par beef nahin khata.* [I have non-veg but not beef.]

– Kindergarten conversations in
Shikshanter, Gurugram

3

'Are we from Pakistan, Mamma?'

'Are we Pakistanis?' Raiqa Saulat Khan felt her eyebrows rising in confusion and anger. Had her son, Faizan, asked this in person, those arched eyebrows would have been all the answer he needed. But they were on the phone, the mother in Bhopal, her son 200 kilometres away in Daly College, Indore.

Through the haze of her emotions, Raiqa had discerned the slight tremble in the voice of her son across the school landline. Raiqa was always quick to pick up such notes, having been attuned to her offspring's every syllable since birth. Yet today she was momentarily unsure, her mother's instinct unable to process what she was hearing. She repeated each word with a weighed paused. 'Are – we – Pakistanis?' Then added, 'Why do you ask?'

His dorm mates at the prestigious boarding

school had said that day, '*Yeh toh atankwadi hain… Yeh toh Pakistani hain…ise maro.* [He is a terrorist. He is a Pakistani. Hit him.]'

It had been just another argument during a basketball game. But the boys had ganged up against Faizan. He was the only Muslim boy in his dorm and he faltered when the sharp accusations came his way. He felt insulted, embarrassed, singled out, cornered and unsure of how to respond.

This was not something he had ever been accused of before. There was no reference point to weigh this against. Why was it said? What did it mean? In his six years in one of the best schools of Bhopal, he had experienced all kinds of boyish banter and bullying. But not this. Why had the word terrorist entered this conversation? Did the boys know something he didn't? Why did they sound so confident?

Raiqa Saulat Khan is an elegant lady in her late forties. She belongs to the extended royal family of the erstwhile state of Bhopal. She lives in a large, old, stone-walled house with high ceilings and fireplaces, located on the grounds of the Ahmedabad Palace.

Daly College, Indore, is steeped in history and family heritage. It was established with donations from ruling families for their scions to study with an entourage of caretakers. Today children of the elite from all over the country study here. Raiqa was only following family tradition when she sent her son to Daly College. Faizan was the third generation of his family to go to this school.

At ten, Faizan was under tremendous pressure to conform, make lasting friendships and be part of this legacy. Yet in a flash he had been branded, made to feel like an outcast. He could sense all eyes on him as he made his way back to his room. He felt anxious, even a little ashamed of committing some unknown crime. It was then that he called his mother. 'Are we Pakistani?' he asked, in a tone laced with anguish and anger. Why had this information been denied him?

Raiqa's outburst left him even more confused. She thundered that they had no ties with Pakistan and she had never even thought of setting foot in the country. Faizan was ready to respect her words and move on but there was a second, more troubling, question. 'Am I a terrorist?'

Raiqa became even more incensed. Had he lost his mind, she bellowed into the phone. How could they be terrorists? They came from an aristocratic family. How could anyone say this to him? The situation was both absurd and deeply painful. At a loss for words, Raiqa reassured her son that she would visit him as soon as possible and continue the conversation in person, and ended the call. Then she broke down and cried.

Raiqa had always taken immense satisfaction in the way she had brought up her kids. They were her pride, her happiness, her strength. But suddenly she felt very weak. She cried as she felt her prestige and her lineage slip from her hands. She felt an intense need to take her son in her arms and protect him. She realized there was nothing she could have done to shield her young son from that experience. She felt alone, very alone.

Raiqa took some time to recover her composure. Then she broke the news to her husband. The next few days saw a lot of back and forth between Bhopal and the school. The school administration was sincerely apologetic and promised that the kids would be asked not to repeat this. The kids were reprimanded and counselled.

'My husband had spent all his student life in the same school and he had never faced this. Some of his closest friends in school were non-Muslims, with their friendship continuing to this day. This was a major turning point in our life. An eye-opener for me as I have been an educationist for the last ten years. So this was all the more shocking to encounter. There were a number of similar ragging incidents after that. We reported the matter to the principal but all he could say was that they are after all kids. We also didn't want to pursue the matter beyond counselling of the students,' says Raiqa.

A few months later, Raiqa and her husband were having lunch with a well-known business family who also had wards in the same school. The talks meandered to Raiqa's work which was at a school on the other side of the town. When she mentioned the location, the other lady gasped. 'But that side means passing through the Mussulman areas!' Her comment elicited an immediate sharp nudge in the arm from her husband. She apologized quickly and said she didn't mean it the way it sounded. Not knowing how to respond, Raiqa smiled weakly. Shortly thereafter, Faizan was withdrawn from the boarding school and brought back to Bhopal.

Back home, they hoped to bury the past. 'I had such a tough time counselling him as he had retreated into a shell. The ragging had started affecting his studies. I know of another boy, Fahd, in a different dorm in the same school who had similar experiences and had to be called back too. We were all so saddened that it has come to this level. All these children were from wealthy business families and royalty.' Back home in Bhopal, Raiqa felt that her son would soon be able to make new friends and move on in life. 'What cannot be cured has to be endured,' she said. But little did she know that even Bhopal had changed.

~

Sanskrit is offered across most of India as an elective third language. Students can opt for it or a regional language or a foreign language. When it's time for the elective language class, the students move out of their sections into different classrooms based on the language they have chosen to study. After the period is over, they return to their class sections.

But something strange is happening in Bhopal. The city has a sizeable Muslim presence so Urdu is offered along with Sanskrit. Since there are a large number of students who take up either language, most Bhopal schools divide up the students of each year into class sections based on the opted languages. So section A will comprise all students who take up Sanskrit and section B those who take up Urdu.

Unlike in most other cities in the country, the segregation by language is thus permanent. When parents questioned this division they were told that timetables are easier to set and students do not need to be shuffled for a single class, and traffic in the school corridors is thus minimized. But when asked officially, school administrations denied the prevalence of any such practices. A school owner, on condition of anonymity, told me, 'It makes economic sense for the administration to group students together according to language. It's easier to set timetables for multiple sections. It's a simple case of maximizing resources. The administrations are only thinking about how much money is being saved.'

Reasonable as this is, its implications are

serious. It means that sections of a class are not only divided along linguistic lines but also end up being divided along religious lines. For, with a few exceptions, the Muslim kids opt for Urdu and the non-Muslim kids opt for Sanskrit. Children hit adolescence in classes 6 to 8 – these are their most formative and impressionable years. When a twelve-year-old child is separated from students of other religions, what are we instilling in them subconsciously?

'I think this compartmentalization of classes started in 2005 in Bhopal,' Raiqa tells me. 'I was vehemently against this when it was introduced in the schools here. I was teaching in one of the leading schools at the time. The majority of the kids in a single section end up being of a single religion. It did have an impact on the kids, as they are not ready to bond with students of other religions. Earlier Faizan had a healthy mix of friends from all religions. But after he came back from boarding school, he has made only Muslim friends. All the kids coming home are Muslims. There is definitely a divide. I can feel it. I can see it.' Raiqa has been a close witness to the changes in Bhopal's society over the years. 'Most of our friends are non-Muslims. My best friend is a Pandit. But my children only have Muslim friends. That worries me,' she says.

I checked with many more parents in Bhopal and most report that kids in the Urdu sections are looked down upon as troublemakers and non-scorers. And therefore the better and 'star' teachers end up teaching the Sanskrit sections. It is difficult to prove and verify these claims but the general sentiment is that Muslims are being pushed into a 'lower-class' position through these means. In Bhopal language is constructing identities literally.

Asma Rizwan, a language instructor and professor of English and business communication in Bhopal, tells me about her IIIT-ian son refusing to sit in an Urdu section because of the labels that would automatically attach to him. He had made deep friendships with a range of children and suddenly in class 6 those friendships were tested by the segregation. For the first time Sameer felt as if he was the 'other'. He refused to take on the uncomfortable burden. He wanted to be in the 'genius' group, the Sanskrit section. He switched subjects in two days.

It was the first day of class in his new section

and roll call was in progress. There is a particular rhythm to the Indian roll call. Once the teacher starts, it's like a train chugging along, each name like a station that it briefly stops at. Roll no. 1… roll no. 2… roll no. 3. 'Ahmad Sameer…' rang out the teacher's voice. He answered, 'Yes ma'am.'

The teacher stopped short, her rhythm broken. She looked up and asked, with a shadow of doubt in her voice, 'Ahmad, you're in the Sanskrit section?' 'Yes ma'am,' came the young student's reply. 'OK, good…very good,' said the teacher and restarted her beat, roll no. 4, roll no. 5, roll no. 6… The teacher had signalled her approval of Sameer's decision, but her pause in the middle of the roll call was an even bigger signal. The point was driven home – Sameer was an outsider, not like the rest of the batch. And this he would be reminded of time and again.

There are few kids like Sameer who leave the Urdu sections and opt for Sanskrit. When sections get further segregated in the senior classes (10–12) between 'achiever' students who score over 90 per cent in their exams and those who don't, the missing Muslim children are further evident. This keeps students from long-term equal achievement, heightens inequality and perpetuates religious rivalry. 'In the morning when you drop your kids you see all students entering the building through the same door,' says a teacher from a leading school in Bhopal. 'But the second door they enter is linguistically or rather religiously graded.'

Students of one section don't get time beyond classes to bond with students from other sections. Raiqa observes, 'If they are compartmentalized this early they don't get to learn about "others". They don't share tiffins. They don't make friends. If you ask the kids, they say, *"Woh bante hi nahin hamare friends. Bas hi-hello ho jata hai.* [They don't become friends with us. We just greet each other in passing.]" This is prevalent in the majority of the schools in Bhopal.'

Various researches in the West have shown clear linkages between racial segregation and academic achievement gaps. Could it hold true for religious segregation too?

The catchment area of one of Delhi's best-known schools includes Jamia and Nizamuddin, two largely Muslim localities. The school offers foreign languages along with Sanskrit and Urdu and one imagines that it would ensure a better balance of religious groups in classes. But a teacher of the school, Ranu Bhogal, tells me, 'My section has mostly Urdu students and a few French students. While it was not an all-Muslim class, the ratio is definitely skewed. So one of the parents wrote a letter to the administration saying they wanted their child's section changed as there was too much of "M factor" [as they put it] in their present section. And they were obliged.'

Many of us grew up being the only Muslim child in a class of forty. But when it's reversed, why does the 'M factor' become a problem? Why does our denominator become only a religious factor to consider? If one parent is obliged, how will you stop all parents from having similar complaints?

Ranu tells me, 'Some very good, well-educated teachers also frequently lament that there are too many "M's" in the school. Some of the Muslim children are from EWS [economically weaker sections] families where, for example, the father is a butcher and the mother is a maid. The teachers are worried that these students might have behavioural issues. As school policy we need to take a percentage of students from the EWS that fall in the school's catchment area. But all the Muslim kids get branded together. Even if the child is good, most of the teachers are biased that all Muslims will behave like the EWS kids. Many teachers refuse to be allotted the Muslim-dominated sections.'

Across India, and especially in the north, any CBSE school that has thirty or more Muslim students in a class clumps them together to form a new section. While such trends in cities are limited to a few schools, smaller towns with large Muslim populations like Darbhanga in Bihar and Moradabad in Uttar Pradesh have begun to implement the same policy as more Muslims embrace formal mainstream English-medium education. We need to talk about the consequences of this beyond classrooms. When a twelve-year-old grows up in classes demarcated on religious lines, how deep will the dividing lines be drawn in our society? Will we ever be able to share a table or a plate? 'Never were differences so open in schools before,' says Raiqa Saulat Khan sadly.

A 2017 survey conducted by the Centre for the Study of Developing Societies (CSDS) revealed that only 33 per cent Hindus count a Muslim among their close friends, whereas 74 per cent

Muslims have a close friend from the Hindu community.[4] The most obvious consequence of this is that the religious majority grow up knowing little about other religions. With the widening divide in schools, this chasm will only deepen further. Today while parents can ensure meals at malls, membership to sports complexes, education at leading institutions and clothes in vogue, what they cannot ensure is that their children will make friends with others beyond their own religious affiliations.

~

Henna: *When I was in junior school, this guy said, 'I will not sit with you. You are a Muslim.'*

Me: *How did you respond to that?*

Henna: *I just kept sitting there.*

– Conversation with Henna,
daughter of a high court judge

---

[4] http://indianexpress.com/article/india/csds-survey-2017-hindus-Muslims-patriotism-close-friends-4600884/

4

On best behaviour

In Bengaluru, thirty-four-year-old Sumaiyah was watching over her three boys aged six, ten and twelve on a lazy afternoon. Outside, the temperatures were soaring, so keeping the feisty little boys inside was a task. After spending time in the splash pool, they were busy with their Xbox. A neighbour, Karan, had joined them and the four were absorbed in a game involving guns, bombs and crackling walkie-talkies. Suddenly Karan jumped up in excitement and screamed at the eldest of the three boys, 'Ayaan, you are a pro at bombing your way out, yaar!' The boys had successfully gone up to the next level in their game.

In the adjoining room a horrified Sumaiyah sat alone hearing the chatter of the boys. Once Karan had left, she told Ayaan not to play any games that were violent again. 'But everyone is playing them, Amma!' complained Ayaan. 'You are not everyone.

And I don't want to ever hear your name and bomb or guns in the same sentence again,' she rebuked, as a confused and upset Ayaan walked away.

What she had failed to convey was her fear that people would brand her child as someone coming from a violent and perhaps extremist family. Didn't everyone expect them to be so? Deep down she knew she was overreacting. But it was an over-reaction she perhaps shared with many Muslim parents.

Farah Jamee, a blogger and one-time journalist, had recently shifted to Gurugram after her husband's transfer from Hyderabad. The house hunt extended beyond the fifteen-day relocation time given by the employers. Farah and her husband took a month and a half instead. They had been well warned of the difficulties a Muslim family would have finding a decent apartment on rent. Farah had therefore given clear guidelines to the property broker: 'Please ensure the landlords are OK with Muslim tenants, only then will we go there to check out the place.' Not one to be easily intimidated, she was always upfront about her identity.

Yet actually living through the drill was a bit

too unreal, a bit too humiliating and a bit too daunting. 'It's not about dealing with one or two stereotypes, there is a truckload. Add to it the present political climate. People just don't want trouble. I can somewhat understand their predicament too,' says Farah.

They finally found a suitable house and moved in. A good school in the vicinity also accepted their four-year-old son, Raed. They were finally beginning to settle down. 'One fine day, I suddenly heard my son say, "I want to go to Pakistan. Pakistan is a good place." I was stunned! I stopped whatever I was doing to pay more attention to what Raed was saying. He kept repeating, "I want to go to Pakistan. When will we go to Pakistan?" I nudged my husband and we both exchanged a worried glance,' says Farah.

She couldn't fathom where Raed had picked up the word Pakistan from. The television had not yet been installed in their new flat, nor did she and her husband discuss politics in front of the boy. Raed had also always been accompanied by her in the new city. Farah began to obsess over this. She tracked back Raed's movements in the past few weeks to understand how the word Pakistan could have slipped into the four-year-old's vocabulary and in what context. Yet she only ended up with dead ends.

'I ignored it that first day, hoping it would stop. But the next day he again started repeating the same lines. This time I got very worried as his new school session was starting the next day. I didn't want him to say such things in front of his new teachers, classmates or even in the neighbourhood. I felt unsettled. We are always on the back foot, trying not to make mistakes. There is always this apprehension inside of us. We don't know how people around us will perceive us or what they might do about it. After all, we had got this flat on rent after tremendous efforts.'

Farah's stable life, so carefully built up, suddenly felt jeopardized. She had no idea why her son was babbling about Pakistan. The more she thought about it, the more confused and worried she became. 'The only thing I could figure was that I had been discussing the need for a new wardrobe for myself and mentioned my love for Pakistani suits in the Delhi heat. Maybe he picked up the word from there. I kept fretting and fretting over this. I couldn't sleep at night, had headaches that wouldn't go away!' she says.

Farah couldn't even ask Raed not to talk about it. There was the possibility of the little boy saying, 'My mummy has asked me not to.' So it was a catch-22 situation. While driving back from the grocery store, Farah finally decided to take the bull by the horns. 'I asked him what was this Pakistan he was referring to. Was it a fruit? Was it a new toy? Or maybe a cartoon or a book? Raed was thoroughly confused at this line of questioning. He gave me a bewildered look as if to say "Mummy you've gone bonkers!" But he didn't have an answer and then never uttered the word Pakistan again. I was so relieved!'

~

A form of self-censorship has crept into our lives. 'Well, I have warned my child to be extra careful with jokes at airports, etc. as nothing is a joke if you are Muslim,' says Sana Hamaad, founder of a digital payments start-up in Mumbai. A Muslim is mostly overconscious at an airport not to say words like bomb or hijack even by mistake or in jest to avoid drawing unnecessary attention and maybe even pre-emptive arrest.

Similarly, Muslim parents try to discourage in their children any behaviour that might stereotype them. We are acutely made aware of prejudices through media, and are always on guard. It is like practising a version of psychological inoculation – exposing our children to biases to protect, or if needed prepare, them from facing bigotry later. Today's parenting includes providing children with a script on how to behave and what to do if they're recognized as a Muslim.

Sana says that her eight-and-a-half-year-old son, Omar, came home from school one day and recounted this conversation with his long-time friend:

Friend: Hey, do you eat beef?

Omar: What? Are you mad?

Friend: My mother has instructed me not to eat anything from your tiffin.

Omar: So what are you fussing about? Simply don't eat my tiffin.

Though Omar had dealt with this lunch-break conversation rather smartly, it left Sana scared

– what if the other kid believed that Omar did indeed have beef? What if he tattled about it? 'It is scary but painfully our reality. Obviously I had to tell my kid that next time just say...we *don't* have beef.' There is no space for open-ended conversations today.

Saira Parveen, a young college pass-out who wears a hijab and abaya, says she watches how she is conducting herself in public. 'Of late, even friends and family have started asking me not to wear my abaya while I travel to non-Muslim localities, which basically means travelling to most areas of Delhi.' This kind of fear cuts through class and region.

One Eid, Hassan, a seven-year-old in Bengaluru, was asked by his father not to wear the traditional kurta-pyjama when he went to play downstairs. His father is a senior software engineer and his mother is a banker and they live in one of the multistoreys dotting the Cambridge layout area. Hassan's father said, '*Thodi der pehno aur phir utar do.* You don't know, *mahaul bada kharab hai.* [Wear it for a while and then take it off. You don't know, these are bad times.]'

Hassan's parents had shifted into this house just

over a year ago, although they had been living in the locality for the past decade. In the new house, Hassan had immediately made friends with a large group of boys. This gave him a new-found sense of freedom and independence as he began to go out alone to play in the community park with them. He also started picking up new things very fast. One day his mother noticed that the boys were making cricket teams and Hassan was told to be in the 'Pakistani' team.

'My son was offended and started shouting, "No, I am not Pakistani!" I was deeply shocked at the deep demarcations. I told the boys that they can instead make teams based on IPL ones.'

Another time, when Hassan was having a fight with one of the boys, the latter complained to his parents about Hassan, referring to him as 'that Muslim boy'. Hassan's mother says, 'I told them that Hassan too has a name and can be addressed by it. I tried to make it about manners. Most of the other families seemed not to reprimand the children. So I ended up taking the de facto counsellor position, and talked to the children as I don't want my child to be rejected, bullied or even worse.'

These everyday biases while building up a slow, simmering resentment still left Hassan and his parents ill prepared for what was to follow. One day Hassan came back early from the playground and told his mother that one of the neighbourhood boys had his birthday party and everyone was going for it. His mother was surprised as she didn't remember the party being mentioned before. Hassan insisted that all his friends were going and had asked him to get ready too. A little while later the friends trooped into Hassan's house and took him along.

Shortly afterwards Hassan came back home crestfallen. He went to the balcony overlooking the neighbour's where his friends had gathered. They shouted asking Hassan why he had left the birthday party. 'Hassan just stood there looking very sad, he didn't have an answer. He himself didn't know why he wasn't there at the party with his friends. When I asked him what happened, he said his neighbour had stopped him from entering the house and had sent him back. At that moment I realized why I had not heard of the party invitation. My son had not been invited,' says his mother.

The parents didn't pursue the matter as they weren't sure about what had happened. 'I thought maybe they'd had a fight or something – after all in such a good neighbourhood it couldn't be anything else. We took our son out to the mall that evening. A few days later, when the birthday boy was playing in our house with Hassan, I asked him what happened. He answered that his mother had instructed him to not invite Hassan as *"Woh log humse different hain, hum unhe nahin invite kar sakte. Woh chhota hai toh saara cake bhi kha jayega.* [Those people are different and so we cannot invite them. Hassan is also too young and might eat all the cake.]"

'I was shocked. The real intentions were clear. Probably my neighbours didn't know their son used to come to our place often instead of going to the playground. Similarly I had never noticed earlier if my child went to their house or not. We were concerned that if they could do this, they might harm him too. So we have been more careful ever since,' says Hassan's mother.

It is almost impossible for a new parent not to worry about how our children will negotiate their way through these varying shades of

Islamophobia and hate. I feel immense relief for having chosen the middle path in naming my child. When someone asks me for my daughter's name, I revel in it being a non-marker. I feel I have unburdened her. And in the process unburdened my own self. But I know no matter what I do she will be marked in school. Should I protect her for as long as I can? After all, how do you tell a child that she is a Muslim and some people might hate Muslims?

Asma Rizwan had recounted a funny story to me as I sat in her white-bougainvillea-lined garden over a cup of coffee in Bhopal. They had shifted to this house when Asma was very young. She was excited about making new friends, meeting new neighbours and exploring the new colony. It was their first day and while the adults were unpacking she sauntered outdoors only to be greeted by an inquisitive face on the boundary wall. She skipped towards the neighbour, happy to answer his many queries on where they had come from and who they were. '*Tum Mussulman ho?* [Are you Muslim?]' suddenly he asked. 'NO! *Tum hoge Mussulman, main toh Asma hoon* [You may be Muslim; I am Asma],' came the indignant retort.

We laughed and I asked when the semantics of the name had registered. 'I did not realize I was a Muslim till I was much older, but it came more quickly to my kids,' she said with a sigh thinking of her son's move to the Sanskrit section at school.

~

Sameer was now at the prestigious IIIT Bangalore. His mother says, 'There he lost sixteen kilos in the first year as he couldn't get used to the mess food. So we asked him to buy a bike so that he could travel to the main city for food.'

Their family is like any other middle-class family that comes from a government service background. Asma's father as well as her husband had worked all their lives in BHEL. The family is filled with doctors, engineers and information technology (IT) professionals and there is an emphasis on a no-frills upbringing of the children and on good education. So the decision to get Sameer a bike was a big, even extravagant, one. Like any college-going young man, Sameer was thrilled with his new possession. It was a simple model, but nevertheless it gave the nineteen-year-old the freedom that he needed from his rigorous studies.

The young man needed to register the new bike, for which he needed a local address. For a hostel student this meant certification from a college authority. When he went to the college registrar, he was told, 'Why should I give you a local address certification? What if you put a bomb on your bike?' Sameer stood still in shock, not believing that this had just been said to him. 'He was so hurt, he called me crying. It badly shook him up. Even if you are a topper and have won the best scholarship you get boxed in the category of jihadists. Sameer could not comprehend why. And I didn't know what to say to him. "Why me?" he kept asking.'

But Sameer's friends supported him and raised their voices against the registrar. Later the hostel warden gave him the certification. The registrar went on to refuse all students address proofs but didn't cite terrorism as a reason for anyone else. 'It kind of shakes you up. It's demeaning, insulting and makes zilch of all your efforts in life. I always told my son that you can shut their mouth only with your result. You have to be extraordinary

– there is no choice. Today my son is the only one from his batch who has been offered a full scholarship in Germany and his university is extremely proud of him,' says Asma.

It was a mini victory over bigotry for the mother and son but they came across it from another quarter later. When Asma applied for Sameer's passport, a local police officer came to their home for the official police verification of address. As Sameer was not at home, Asma requested the police officer to return later. The officer replied that he would and said, '*Ab ma'am Muslim ladke ka case hai toh double inquiry hogi na.* [Ma'am, a Muslim boy requires double inquiry and verification of credentials.]'

Furious, Asma took up the matter with a friend who was a senior police officer and action was taken. The officer apologized for his behaviour and issued the clearance when Sameer came. 'But what if I did not have friends in an influential position?' asks Asma.

With the passport in place, Sameer booked his tickets for Germany. He tried reaching out to other Indians in Germany for a shared space to live for the duration of the internship. Many leads ended up in dead ends. A dejected Sameer shared his worry about not finding accommodation with his younger sister, who studies at NID and has bagged a campus placement at IBM. She recommended that instead of writing his full name 'Ahmad Sameer' perhaps he could write 'A. Sameer' and that the non-religion-specific name would probably get him the response he was looking for. 'So, yes, they are constantly thinking about it in the back of their minds and are constantly working around their identity,' says Asma.

~

Such social anxiety gets heightened by the news that crowds our social media timeline. With so many reports on how Muslims are picked up by the police, shot in fake encounters or are put behind bars with little or no evidence, I can hardly blame our youth for feeling disenfranchised. They don't know why or when they might be picked up. Like my husband, who in college went at 1 a.m. to report a burglary in his rented flat with two other flatmates at the Hauz Khas police station in South Delhi. They were told, 'Now how do I write your report? One of you is called Yasser, the other Saif and the third is Mohammed. I don't know if I should write your report or a report on you.'

They came back without filing a report, scarred for life. They learnt to live with it, internalizing a fear of the system, turning it into a kind of self-censorship. 'What can I google from my laptop or mobile? Can I sell my old bike/car on OLX? Who knows who might buy it and use it for what purpose? Can I ask for water from my neighbour?' From the mundane to the marked, everything goes through a scanner in the head from the viewpoint of being a Muslim. And living the Muslim tag. You cannot run from it. You cannot hide from it. You cannot embrace it.

5

Reluctant fundamentalists

Many young mothers are not prepared for the inner conflict their children might be facing. This often leads to someone else stepping in into the parenting vacuum. Raiqa Saulat Khan worries when Faizan plays violent games on his Xbox. 'Think about it,' she says. 'He has disturbing memories from school where he was called a terrorist, now he has only Muslim friends and then he plays these games. It's not just one thing but a number of things making them violent. We can keep telling them that it is wrong but it's a fine balancing act – about what to allow and what to deprive them of. All we can do is pray and counsel. Also, how do you stop young kids from seeing disturbing visuals like of ISIS beheadings or Muslim lynchings? They get such videos forwarded on WhatsApp. They are young, impressionable, and being pushed into a corner. I think it's a cause for concern. A lot of concern.'

Dr Farrukh Waris retired as the principal of the Burhani College of Arts and Commerce in Mumbai. When her twenty-six-year-old son, Sadayaan, went to study at the Indian School of Business (ISB), the whole family was elated. ISB is one of the most prestigious institutions in India and it was a moment of pride for everyone. When Sadayaan returned home after a few months for his holidays, it was towards the end of Ramzan. He told his mother that he had been fasting through the holy month.

Dr Waris was very surprised. 'I said very good, but who gives you sehri and iftari at ISB?' Sadayaan told her that there were six or seven other Muslim students at ISB and all of them were fasting. So they made a group and each one brought one food item that they shared with the others. These students were from everywhere: London, Australia, all over India. Dr Waris recounts the sudden fear she felt as she heard her son's story. 'I don't like this. Please be afraid, be very afraid. Be frightened of others who are bringing so much of religion to an institution like ISB. Have you checked on their backgrounds? What do we know about them? I don't trust them,' she told her son.

Sadayaan laughed and reassured his mother that all the other mothers of the boys were saying the same thing to their sons. 'They are saying Sadayaan is from Mumbai where the bomb blasts took place. Be careful of him, don't be friends with him. So I realized it is everybody's fear. Of children being exposed to any other brand of Islam than the one we follow,' says Dr Waris.

Dr Waris's colleague, a divorced single mother, had a thirteen-year-old son who suddenly started going to the mosque every day, especially for the early morning Fajr prayers. He told his mother that his peers were doing the same thing. 'That's the first step by his peers – to pull the adolescent child into the masjid by making him feel old enough or man enough to do it. They would say, *"Ab tumhari moochein aane lagi hain. Tumhe toh masjid jana chahiye"* [You have started to grow a moustache. You are old enough to go to the masjid],' says Dr Waris.

Her colleague was very happy that her son had taken to religion so seriously at an early age

– especially as he had no elder male figure in the house. But alarm bells rang in Dr Waris's head. She says, 'When your thirteen-year-old boy goes to the mosque at five in the morning, what kinds of influences is he absorbing? Should any mother expose her young child to outside influences which she has no knowledge of or control over? When I spoke to my colleague about my worries, she immediately put an end to it. Only Friday prayers were allowed in the mosque thereafter. We don't know if there was anything wrong going on at the masjid. Probably not. But why risk it? There is an apprehension in everybody's mind, and if not then there should be.'

Safia Shaikh is the mother of two children. The elder one is a boy who works in marketing and the younger one a girl who is a well-known fashion designer. Yet there is the fear lurking at the fringes of their lives. 'I was dead scared of my son, Usman, becoming a radical because some of his friends were very conservative. Although he is grown-up and married now, I still check on him from time to time. He is active on social media and keeps sharing posts I do not approve of – of atrocities from across the world. Of late he has started sporting a beard. Even his wife got worried then. I got after him to shave. In today's atmosphere one just doesn't know. May our kids always be kept safe, insha Allah.'

Shehla Rafat tells me about a friend who was brought up by atheist parents but has now become very religious. 'He is progressive and lets his wife do her own thing but he himself has become strict about his adherence to what he understands as Islamic diktats. And his wife worries about him crossing the thin line and what it will mean for their children. It's not necessary he will become a rabid Islamist. Even my father was a maulvi but not a rabid Islamist. He was a man of his times, influenced by the ideas of the seventies. But today, how does one know any more?'

Another friend voices her concerns in whispers. Her sister in Pune is in her mid thirties, highly qualified and unmarried. She was suffering from severe depression and low self-esteem. Suddenly she became extremely devout. She started observing strict hijab, talking to people online on Islamic values and brought in and sheltered converts or 'reverts'. She talked of the oppression of Muslims and how the 'kafirs' had succeeded because the Muslims did not follow 'true Islam'. 'I didn't know who she was talking to online but we were all very scared – in her frame of mind it is very easy to influence her.'

While we worry about these shifts in our friends and relatives, most Muslim mothers I spoke to felt especially vulnerable about their children. How does one know which ideas will seem attractive to our children? Especially now, when they are growing up in an atmosphere of increasing intolerance, being bullied about their religion, and are being told to 'go to Pakistan' or called 'terrorist' in the playground.

Senior journalist Sumaira Khan, a mother of two young kids, explains, 'If we see overt signs of religion adopted by the kids then we need to start thinking. Some parents think that it's good that the child has willingly adopted a burkha or has started voluntarily going to jamaat. But this actually means that the child might have come into contact with someone who has led them to this. Once these things start it's an unending tunnel. And it often leads to extremes. They start cutting themselves off from friends. They won't eat at Hindu houses, won't talk to the other sex. Where are these ideas coming from? How was your child exposed to them? It's best to step in almost immediately. When one gets into such circles the first changes come in lifestyle, then in their ideologies and ultimately changed mindsets. It can be a precursor to anything.'

~

Indian Muslims have on the whole been far less involved in terrorism than their counterparts from other countries. A tenth of the world's Muslims live in India yet the ISIS so far is reported to have recruited fewer than seventy people from among India's 172 million Muslims. But this could change.

The group mostly targets those from relatively privileged backgrounds, and this means the urban middle-class Muslim child might be more vulnerable to radicalization than the rural poor. 'It is a tough statement to make. This is not something that is black and white,' says a home ministry official quoted in a recent *Open* article.

The official argues that 'higher awareness – cable TV to the internet – besides physical links with the Gulf, has resulted in significant radicalization among the Muslims of Kerala. This trend might be repeated in other states as well when Muslims reach comparable degrees of social growth and mobility.' He also worries that the 'Muslim bashing' which has become 'common in some politically powerful circles' will only aggravate matters.[5]

It is often argued that dissatisfaction among Indian Muslims has been low as they are the world's most stable and well-integrated minority group. But considering that the fault lines are widening day by day, we need to take a hard look at where we are going. Jihadists usually are able to pull youth in by saying we accept you as you are, you are one of us, you belong here even though the world rejects you. Youth who feel disenfranchised are more susceptible to this pull.

Michael Kugelman, Asia Program Deputy Director and Senior Associate for South Asia at

[5] http://www.openthemagazine.com/article/cover-story/god-s-recruits

the Woodrow Wilson Center, Washington, says Indian government policies have at best put the Indian Muslim community on the defensive and at worst made it apprehensive about its well-being. 'The vulnerability of Muslims is particularly compounded in regions like Uttar Pradesh, where you have top leaders that are explicitly anti-Muslim.'[6]

Of the total number of ISIS recruits identified by the National Intelligence Agency, only a fifth had studied at madrasas; the rest went to regular schools. Many of those involved in international acts of terrorism are known to be well educated. For example, Mohamed Atta (9/11 attacks) had studied architecture at Cairo University and continued his studies in Germany at the Hamburg University of Technology. Ziad Jarrah (9/11 attacks) was born to a wealthy and 'secular' family and had studied aerospace engineering at the Fachhochschule (University of Applied Sciences) in Hamburg. Tamim Chowdhury, the alleged mastermind of the July 2016 Dhaka attacks, was a 'shy, skinny

[6] http://www.openthemagazine.com/article/cover-story/god-s-recruits

kid'[7] who had graduated from the University of Windsor with an honours degree in chemistry. Education certainly does not prevent the creation of ferment in a young Muslim's mind. In today's political climate we have to be concerned about where and how far we are pushing our children. I wonder if the middle-class Indian Muslim parent is scared enough.

The more the resistance we face from the outside world, the more our consciousness of being Muslim increases. Those who grow up in the Gulf tell me how they became acutely aware of being Muslim only after they went outside the Middle East. 'When my family shifted back to India, it was the first time I said, "I am a Muslim." I realized I had never had to say that out aloud before,' says architect Sana Khan. 'I was reminded more of it by my extended family here.'

---

[7] Alex Migdal, 'Bangladeshi Terror Group Affiliated with IS Reportedly Led by Canadian', 2 July 2016, *The Globe and Mail*, Toronto. https://beta.theglobeandmail.com/news/world/bangladeshi-terror-group-affiliated-with-is-reportedly-led-by-canadian/article30733718/?ref=http://www.theglobeandmail.com& (retrieved 11 July 2016).

Everyone has multiple identities. For me, the least important identity is that I am an Allahabadi as I have lived at various places. Being a mother is an important identity. Being a woman and being a Muslim are also very important. Being an Indian is the most important identity. But all these identities are seldom spelt out in life. And yet, the one identity that every child does grow up hearing repeatedly is that of being a Muslim – both from the world outside and from within the community.

6

Haraam police

Zuveria Ali was busy preparing for her son's first birthday. It had to be a grand affair. After all, he was the son of the editor-in-chief of one of Hyderabad's oldest and most popular Urdu newspapers. No stone would be left unturned. As she put up the last of the decorations in place, she felt a sense of pride. Her son would have a memorable first birthday. It was a big moment – how quickly the year had passed. She picked up the 'Happy Birthday' streamer and put it up on the wall. Next to it she put up her son's name, Mohammad. Satisfied, she stepped back to take a look and was horrified at what she saw. The streamer read 'Happy Birthday Mohammad'.

She had grown up being told that birthday celebrations were wrong and not allowed in Islam. So how could she use 'Mohammad' in a birthday party banner? It felt borderline blasphemous.

What would the haraam police say? Zuveria decided to remove 'Mohammad' and use her son's second name instead on the wall.

The 'haraam police' is a common feature in most Muslim lives. It is that someone in the family or extended family who polices your every action or inaction through a myopic Islamic lens. There is always a degree more of conservatism to compete with. The Islam practised today is like the stereotypical mother in private – consoling, reassuring, calming – but like the stereotypical mother-in-law in public – always making you feel you haven't lived up to expectations. Thus most of us end up living under the fear of being rejected by the custodians of the faith which is what the haraam police believes itself to be.

Today just as we must wear our nationalism on our sleeve for the world outside, similarly we have to wear Islam on our sleeve inside the community. There is no tolerance on either side. On one side, we are increasingly being reminded of our Muslim identity. And yet, in our homes within the larger Muslim community, we are often told that we are not Muslim enough. Our children too are caught in this impossible vortex.

Dr Farrukh Waris says, 'My younger girl Anam's birthday was around the corner and she went around distributing the invitation cards. We had only one Muslim neighbour in the building. Their five-year-old kid opened the door and said to my girl, "We don't celebrate birthdays." So Anam being Anam said, "OK, you don't come if you wish but I will celebrate my birthday."'

A few months later, a new help, Manisha, came looking for work to Dr Waris's house and she was hired for kitchen work and cleaning. After a few weeks she saw Dr Waris offering namaz, and said, '*Allah! Tum Mussulman ho? Magar uparwali ne bola ki tum Mussulman nahin ho, isliye maine apna naam doosra bola, main bhi Mussulman hoon. Mera naam Aneesa hai jise maine Manisha kar diya!* [You are Muslim too? But the lady above said that you are not a Muslim. That is why I changed my name. I am also a Muslim. My name is Aneesa that I changed to Manisha!]' Dr Waris tells me that the 'uparwali' was the same neighbour and they were making a point about how Islamic they were as they had begun wearing the burkha and hijab.

A few weeks later the neighbour visited Dr Waris and asked if she would 'come to a mehfil'. On asking what would happen there, the neighbour responded, 'They will bring you to the right path. See, you don't wear a burkha, then how will your girls wear it and how will your daughters-in-law wear it. If you wear it, then on the day of judgement your face will be luminous and your body will be shining. There are so many virtues of wearing the burkha.' Dr Waris patiently heard her through and then asked where the mehfil was taking place. To which the neighbour proudly answered, 'I go to Pali Hill. *Aur wahan Saira Bano bhi aati hain.* [Saira Bano, the legendary film actress, also comes there.]'

~

Elahe Hiptoola, a renowned film producer in India, tells me, 'I am a hardcore Shia-Bohri Muslim. It is also something very cultural for me. When I was once in the Khan El-Khalili bazaar in Egypt, I realized that the Al-Hussain Mosque was nearby where we believe Imam Hussain's head is buried. I left my friends behind as I didn't want them to see me getting emotional which I do when I enter such a holy place. In the historic mosque, I felt overwhelmed and started crying. Just then I noticed another woman in a rida [the Bohri burkha]. I was overjoyed to see a fellow Bohri Muslim and I reached out to her and told her that I too was a Bohri. Her response was the exact opposite of what I was feeling. Instead of sharing my joy, she looked upset. She informed me angrily that I should be in a burkha, not in the skirt and T-shirt I was wearing. I was like… hello, I am in Hussain's mazaar. At least respect that! But all she cared about was the farmaan and the burkha.'

I can relate with Elahe's feelings very well. The first time I came to Delhi, I went on a tour of the beautiful Mughal monuments. It was a blistering hot day and I was wearing a kurta over my jeans. We reached Jama Masjid when it was time for namaz and I said my prayers in the women's section. Suddenly, a woman sitting next to me tugged at my sleeve and said, '*Namaz qubool nahin hogi tumhari* [God will not accept your prayers].' She had disapproval and disgust written all over her face. I was young and this was probably the first time I was praying outside my house. The tranquillity of the mosque was marred by the woman's disapproval and the ugly moment has stayed etched in my mind. I didn't go to pray in the Jama Masjid for nearly a decade thereafter.

'I think today being Muslim is more of a fight one has to have with one's own family, relatives and extended community rather than the people around. There is always the background noise telling us what to do or how to be a better Muslim in every aspect of daily life. One has to work this out in one's own personal space than with the rest of the world. Life is often easier outside,' says Shehla Rafat.

Noted writer and literary historian Rakhshanda Jalil's younger daughter Insha had another Muslim classmate in school. They had been in school together since nursery. When the girls hit adolescence, around class 8, the other girl started wearing salwar kameez instead of a skirt as part of her school uniform (the school gave options for the same). Later, she started to wear the hijab too. So all their friends who they had grown up with started to ask Insha, 'You both are Muslims, then why are you so different?' Insha would respond that every human is different and so were the two of them. But the other girl would say to her friends that Insha didn't know anything about Islam, which is why she didn't cover her hair and so she wasn't a true Muslim.

Often Muslims don't mix with other Muslims in urban areas fearing they'd be judged for not 'being Muslim enough'. This is especially true for working women. IT professional and mother of two young boys, Romana Siddiqui says, 'Somehow I never felt comfortable when living in an all-Muslim neighbourhood. I could never be myself, especially in terms of dressing, and always had to behave in a certain way. I was quick to be given labels.'

The children absorb this nervousness and grow up being told in various ways that he or she is just not Muslim enough. Blogger Rukhsar Saleem says that while growing up there was always the gossip that she and other girls in her family were not 'so Muslim' because they were outspoken and outgoing. Respected journalist and author from Assam, Teresa Rehman says, 'I feel uneasy in Muslim gatherings. There are always the snide remarks about women. There is always this fear of not being traditional enough. Ultimately many of these converge around covering your hair.'

Just as hijabis are often ostracized or treated differently outside the community, the non-hijabis are attacked within. It is easy to put women in a veil and forget that the Quran first puts the onus on a man to lower his gaze. The weight of modesty lies on the men and not entirely on the women. Instead the hijab is often used as a benchmark by conservative Muslims to judge the morality of a Muslim woman and her 'Muslimness'.

This puts pressure on both the sides to conform to the identity. Modern women who took to the hijab as a personal free choice often find themselves deflecting negative portrayal of their hijabs by going the extra mile. Asiya Ahmed Khan, a naturalist who wears the hijab, was worried about the impressions it would have on her daughter as she grew up. What if her daughter, Maryam, turned around one day and told her that she was stuck in traditions while the world had moved on?

'So I knew I had to set the right examples. I was never dependent on anyone in spite of my hijab. It was always I who changed the light bulb at home. I made space for myself in my line of work outside the home. I can go anywhere alone and talk to anyone. I drive, I have done well in my studies, I do all the household shopping, I do all the repairs around the house from the kettle to the television. I made sure I put up an example for my daughter that didn't make her feel I had not achieved anything because of my hijab. I never quit,' says Asiya.

Similarly, those who do not wear the hijab find themselves putting the extra effort in front of their children to dispel any thoughts of them being lesser Muslims. My daughter is still very young to question, but I am sure I would want her to grow up with stories of how the 'ideal woman of Islam' Hazrat Khadija, the first wife of Prophet Mohammad (PBUH), was a businesswoman par excellence and how her business made as much money as all the other traders of her tribe made together. Instead of growing up on stories of wrongly placed values, like how a perfect Muslimah is one with a hijab which gives her respect. Respect or self-esteem does not need external validation.

'As a secular Indian it wasn't a rough ride until now. But as a practising Muslim it was always a rough ride. Celebrating a birthday? You are not a Muslim. You are not wearing a hijab? You are not a Muslim. You are not going for istemaas or dars? You are a lesser Muslim and so on. There are a thousand things in everyday life that make it a rough ride,' says Dr Waris.

Rakhshanda Jalil says, 'The Muslim community will never accept you as one of their own until and unless you have surrendered every vestige of your own individuality. Any form of individuality is a no-no. For a woman, if your head is uncovered or your sleeves aren't full, you will not be accepted. Patriarchy is a devil in itself but when patriarchy gets mixed with religion, it is a very potent mixture.'

While girls often have it worse, boys are not spared either. A leading television journalist says, 'Our father was of an argumentative nature and would debate with us on all topics, including religion. I grew up seeing the mullahs shrug off his debates and call him an unbeliever. Just because he questioned everything. We always heard that one was not supposed to question. But because we always had questions in our minds, we felt we were not the typical Muslim kids around. Anything unconventional was not welcome. Later when I went into journalism, for a good decade I was made to feel I had done a great misdeed, as I was on television, the first from my home town. It is only very recently that the same people have begun asking me how to get their kids into journalism.'

We as a community are fussing so much over the details that we are blindsiding the larger picture. All our beef is with pedantic rituals and we don't look at our civic issues, education or aspirations. We must learn from the examples across the world. Because without course correction, the next generation will become easy breeding ground for radicalization. We have to be worried when children grow up with destination akhrat, the Day of Judgement, in mind while at the same time they are being alienated and bullied in schools and workplaces. I wonder, how did we get here?

7

How did we get here?

'Let me take you back half a century to when Muslim identities were not pasted all over us as it is now,' says Dr Farrukh Waris. She lives in the bylanes of a tree-lined Parsi colony in Bandra. As I enter her home, almost a century-old wooden two-storey building, history seems to whisper to me. Dr Waris is an ever-smiling, grey-haired lady with one of the sweetest voices I have ever heard. Her home is a mirror of her: soft, warm and cosy. I settle down quickly into her story.

Dr Waris remembers, 'In the mid to late sixties, when petro-dollars became a reality, Saudi Arabia and the Middle East threw open their gates to Muslims. Most came back learning Wahhabism and Salafism [two ultra-conservative sects of Islam]. Women did not accompany them in the early days and absorbed open-mouthed what the men brought back from the great land that housed the revered cities of Mecca and Medina. There was complete veneration of all these ideas, and of course the money pouring in amplified everything.

'I remember till the seventies the idea of securing a place in Jannạt wasn't widely accepted in India. After the eighties it seemed to have become the sole purpose of being a Muslim. Everything is for akhrat. Many of my cousins who went to Saudi in the eighties came back as mullahs. Men who went clean-shaven and wearing well-tailored pant suits, came back fifteen years later bearded, with topis, and with their wives and daughters in hijabs. It changed the complete profile of the family. Islam was engraved all over their psyche with *tauba tauba* all the time.

'We said to them, *"Arre tum toh bade Mussulman ho gaye, hum bhi hain, par tum kis kisam ke Mussulman ho gaye?* [You have become very religious, we are also Muslims, what type of Muslim have you become?]" The whole family was aghast. And they would talk about Islam to us as if they were educating non-Muslims! It was almost a daawat-e-Islam: *"Hum daawat de rahein hain Islam qubool karne ke liye* [We are inviting you to accept Islam]." It felt weird and uncomfortable as most of it was about maintaining appearance. *Pyjama kitna chhota hona chahiye, aastee in kitni lambi honi chahiye* [How short your pants should be or how long your sleeves must be], etc. The people who had stayed back in India and were not dependent on them for money were not impressed at all. We thought these Gulf-returnees expressed a rigidity of thought.'

Many families across India have similar stories to recount. As the Saudi economy grew with the petroleum industry, so did its influence over all things 'Islam'. Dr Waris's father had settled down in Aligarh and had a South Indian help named Vasudevan. Her mother had died long ago and all the siblings were married and settled outside Aligarh. So Vasudevan was the only one who looked after her father full-time. One day a Gulf-returned cousin, Sallan bhai, called up her father and told him that he was coming back to India after many years and wished to stay with his uncle for about a week.

Dr Waris's father was delighted by the news and looking forward to meeting his nephew and the grandchildren. Then a while later Sallan bhai called back and said, '*Mamujaan, hamein pata laga hai ki aapke paas ek Hindu naukar hai, toh hamare khane ka kya hoga...hum khana kaise khayenge?* [Mamujaan, we have just come to know that you have a Hindu cook, so what about our food? How will we eat?]'

Dr Waris's father was utterly shocked. He asked his nephew what the problem was. The nephew said he and his family would not eat anything cooked by a Hindu. Vasudevan had been Dr Waris's father's right-hand man for decades; he was part of the family. Dr Waris's father replied, '*Toh miyan main yahi kahoonga ki aap mere paas mat aaiyega. Kyunki main Vasu miyan ke ahsasaat ko majrooh karoonga nahin lekin main aapke khayalat se wakayi majrooh ho chuka hoon. Toh aapse ilteja karoonga ki aap directly Allahabad chale jayiyega, Aligarh mat rukiyega. Agar zindagi rahi toh main aapse kabhi Allahabad mein mil loonga.* [I will only say this: don't come to me. Because I will not hurt the sentiments of Vasudevan but I am very offended by your views. So I will request you to go to Allahabad directly and not stop in Aligarh. If all goes well, I will meet you in Allahabad.]'

'So my cousin had been trying to earn brownie points but it backfired… It was all clearly about trying to be a bigger Muslim than the other,' explains Dr Waris.

What about the children of such people? Over the past few decades this rigidity has not just spread but has also been handed down. It manifests itself in many ways. Especially since many madrasas began to be funded by these same petro-dollars. Writer Sehba Imam remembers, 'In Aligarh, in our early childhood days, the masjids were somehow never too close to the kind of places we lived in. A strain of azan would float by unobtrusively, through the playground, indicating the time to go home. *"Maghrib ki azan se pehle ghar aa jana"* [Come home by the evening azan] used to be the standard instruction from Mom. Masjids were few and far between. For years, the only masjid I knew was a quaint, faded pink, single-minar structure called Ek Minar ki Masjid. It was on the way to the qabristan and I was both scared and fascinated by it. Once when a friend asked us to go in with him, I ran back the moment my feet touched the cold marble floor. I don't remember if it had a loudspeaker those days.

The azan was an alarm clock for parents, a curfew to get back home for us kids, a segue into night after a cluttered day filled with school, friends and random visits from relatives – it was a lot of things to a lot of people – but never a war cry or an announcement of faith.'

With time as the town started spreading beyond the university or old quarters, masjids started sprouting up everywhere. Sehba remembers how they seemed to grab breathing spaces between houses and screamed for attention. Some were a blinding white; some looked like they had been dropped in a tub of loud green by mistake. Many grown-ups at that time scoffed and complained about Gulf money.

'While earlier one single familiar voice of the muezzin wafted across the area, knitting many mohallas together, gently inviting or marking time, now azans barged into homes from many directions. Loudspeakers amplified the harshness of untrained muezzins. These were not artists but more like raw zealots. There was more passion than reverence in their voices. We giggled, laughed, poked fun at them and called them *phata baans* [broken musical instruments]. Devout aunties covered their heads when they heard the discordant sound. No one judged us for laughing at the muezzins and covering our ears or for running indoors and shutting the door to keep the noise out. Religion was not a live bomb that could go off at the slightest touch of irreverence. You were free not to share their enthusiasm without being branded as an enemy of faith,' Sehba says.

~

'My son started learning his Quran when he was four years old,' remembers Ayesha Bilgrami from Hyderabad. Over breakfast, we talk of being a Muslim in the world today. Works of M.F. Husain casually grace every wall of her flat in Banjara Hills. I wondered if they were copies till the personalized inscriptions caught my eye. There is a beautiful carved swing in the middle of the wide hall. I haven't seen a house done with more flair for the arts and without being ostentatious.

I hear the tinkering in the kitchen as breakfast is put together. The man of the house comes in and I say my salaams and apologize for intruding into their home on a beautiful Sunday morning. He dismisses my apologies with a wave. An amused curiosity lights up his eyes as he settles in at the table, giving his wife the space directly opposite to me.

Ayesha continues, 'So the maulvi saheb was a gentle old fellow who would come and sit in the veranda. We had this hat rack with various kinds of headwear, my father-in-law's bowler hat, a sun hat, straw hat, berets and many riding caps as we all used to ride. So my son, Saif, decided that he would study only if maulvi saheb wore a hat that Saif chose for him. Maulvi saheb's traditional topi wouldn't do. Saif wouldn't allow the white skullcap! So every day maulvi saheb would end up wearing a different cap...a straw hat one day...a bowler hat on another day. It used to be so funny. Maulvi saheb would come in and eye the hat rack quietly thinking, *Aaj main kya banoonga*? [What will I be today?]'

We tumble into heaps of laughter as we settle at the breakfast table. She shows me a black-and-white picture of a little boy reading his Quran with a bearded maulana in a large hat. I tell Ayesha apa that this is the funniest thing I have ever seen. One cannot imagine a maulana being so flexible. 'Yes, he was a sweet one. Though the ones nowadays are very rigid.' I let that sink in.

I am reminded of a summer I spent at my nana's bungalow when I was very young. What made this holiday special was that the youngest and the oldest of the six mamus had come together after a long time. The oldest mamu, having worked and lived in Mecca, had taken on the responsibility of upholding the religiousness of the khandan upon himself. The youngest did what the young do best. And on this particular day, he was sleeping on one of the charpoys. The house was like a wondrous maze to my little girl eyes. It was a jigsaw of endless rooms connected by narrow, winding staircases, and unending rooftops. The men of the house, including my elder brother and a few other cousins and older men, camped out in the veranda on charpoys in the heat.

At Fajr time, Mamujaan, as we lovingly yet fearfully called our eldest mamu, woke up, got ready, and called out to the rest of the men who were in deep slumber. His voice boomed in the narrow, whitewashed veranda, '*Chalo utho, namaz ka waqt ho gaya* [Wake up, it's time for the morning prayer].'

All of you will agree that studying in convent schools makes us inherently goody-two-shoes. And at the first boom of Mamujaan's voice, my brother shot up, washed and dressed up within a matter of minutes. As the two men proceeded towards the door, Mamujaan turned towards the sleeping men and boomed out one last time, 'See this very young boy can get up to accompany me for the prayers, but you all cannot! I hope you feel ashamed of yourself? *Sharam aati hai ya nahin??* [Aren't you ashamed?]'

The youngest mamu slowly raised his head, a mop of glossy black curls, opened one bleary eye and drawled, '*Ji, sharam aa gayi* [Yes, I feel ashamed].' The head then fell back on to his pillow. Legend goes that my brother for the first time saw an angry old man in prayer.

As we grew up and started to understand the need of both humour and religion, we realized that humour in matters of religion had become a scarce commodity.

~

It is Bakr Eid. I am in Jamia Nagar in Delhi. The day often means chaos on the streets in Muslim neighbourhoods. As I make my way along the roads, careful of where I step, I hear an unfamiliar sound. I have heard enough goats bleating but this is different. I turn towards the source of the sound. In a vacant plot of land sandwiched between two multistorey houses a camel lies tied down. I inquire what's happening and a bystander tells me, '*Oonth laaye hain Khan saheb zibaah karne ke liye* [Khan saheb has got a camel to sacrifice].'

I watch as hilarity ensues. No one knows how to sacrifice the tall and healthy camel. The camel refuses to stay still and accommodate the men trying to kill it. In the tussle he lets out some dreadful screams. That is what I had heard. More people join in to see the tamasha. Some coax the camel. Others coax the men. I decide I have had enough and leave the show.

As I walk away I realize this is exactly what is happening everywhere. The camel is indigenous to Saudi Arabia and camel meat is a delicacy in that part of the world. But in India it is not so. We are bringing in what's right for the Saudis in a geography and culture that are vastly different in context. The Islam we have was culturally syncretic with the Indian Ganga-Jamuni tehzeeb. It is fast eroding in the face of religious conservatism. Islamophobia in the garb of nationalism is accelerating this erosion leaving behind a confused generation.

It's no more the elephant in the room. Conservative Islamization and rabid Islamophobia today are the twin camels we cannot tame.

8

Epilogue

One of my oldest memories is of my mother's low, melodious voice reading the Quran as Maghrib approached. It would gently flow as the sky changed its colour. As if her deep, undulating rhythm was enough to pull the whole world into a deep slumber. Her voice remains embedded in my mind.

The magical quality of the voice would beckon us from wherever we were playing much like Pied Piper. We would giggle as Mamma closed her Quran and gently blew through her pursed lips the dua into our faces and inside our clothes. We wore her dua as an invisible vest around us and felt comforted in its warmth.

Today Myra has begun to show signs of independence. She is already in playgroups and is ever ready to go explore the world outside. Slowly, step by step, month by month, she is letting go of my fingers to find her own footing. I understand now, as a parent myself, why my mother read the religious scriptures and blew her prayers on us. It was her way of keeping us safe when she wasn't around. I too find myself giving Myra my own dua vests. Because mothers cannot be everywhere.

But our prayers and words can always accompany our children, subconsciously become the voice in their heads. I try to take a long, hard look at my own words to know how my child will process the world around her. She will see this world as joyful and as happy a place as I tell her it is. She will find it as wondrous as my words paint the world to be. She will also find it as dark as the many demons I tell her are out there waiting for her.

I have not introduced the concept of ghosts to little Myra, and she is unafraid to skip into any dark room alone. With no fear holding her back, she simply reaches out and switches on the lights. We live in a nuclear family in a cosmopolitan society where not everyone knows their neighbours. It is a controlled environment, and easy to gatekeep information reaching my three-year-old. But some day someone will tell her, 'Oh, but it's dark, won't you be afraid?' and from there the journey to the dark world of fears will start for my Myra. She will learn that she is expected to be afraid. Just as a casual remark about a news story on Hindus–Muslims might throw up differences with negative connotations for her to process.

Once she reaches the world of the big school, the task of gatekeeping will become even harder. There will be many who will tell her about demons that exist and there will be many monsters that I too will have to warn her about to protect her from physical harm. But while working on this book, I realized there is a mental and emotional harm that we mothers have not been preparing them for. The task gets only more difficult as they grow up and their avenues of information increase – television, social media, peers and other adults.

This book only mirrors the world we have created for our children. In truth, it is not the words of the kids that hurt. It's the imagined words in the speech of the parents and other adults around the kid that hurt more. What are we saying in our drawing rooms and over dinner tables which our kids translate into hatred for each other in classrooms and playgrounds? If we truly look into our own hearts, and listen to our politicians and journalists with open minds, we will find the source.

It is easy not to care from a majoritarian perspective. It is easy to mentally distance yourself from all that is happening around by tagging it as the fringe or letting it play out in the name of politics. By doing so you fail us, the nation-loving Muslims who are fast becoming the collateral damage. My own family had funded the 1857 revolt, the men of my family were hanged from the neem trees at Allahabad chowk by the British. My family never gave up fighting for our India. Neither will I.

My 'authentic Muslim woman' right now is battling the only identity being granted to her. That is of being only a Muslim. She is fighting so that this identity is not pushed on to her children too. We have to be careful of the stereotypes we allow to be created in the minds, hearts and psyche of our youth. They will be what they think they should be.

All of us, from all religions, need to recognize the challenges of the twin evils of hatred and rigidity that are facing us. While men easily become political pawns, it is the need of the hour for women to rise. We are here, this is ours, and we are a part of the story that is India. I truly, honestly believe there is no place that could give us the best of all worlds like India does. This is our home, our mother and we fight for it with our children. We owe it to our Allah. We owe it to our India.

Because there is still hope.

There is always hope.

Acknowledgements

To the friends we have lost over the past few years. You made the hurt closer to home.

To the innumerable women who opened their hearts, homes and memories for me. I can still smell your coffee, still hear your laughter, still feel your pain. I will live with the many more stories that we could not include in these pages. Thank you.

My editor, Chiki Sarkar, who took this baby of mine and nursed it as her own. Who shared my heartbreak and tears over the stories and helped turn around the text with a clearer perspective and gave it a solid direction.

Priya Ramani, for believing in the idea and beginning this journey. Farhatullah Beig bhai and Asma Rizwan apa for having homes made up entirely of love and laughter and open for everyone. Thank you for making me a part of them for a few days as I travelled to unknown cities for my research. Meenakshi Jauhari, for always being there and never saying no. For helping me be the woman I am and championing the book's cause. Abhay Chawla, for backing my 'brilliant ideas' always and letting me get away without seeing them through. This book is in lieu of all those times. Tejas Saini for being Myra's first best friend. Raveen for taking care of the kids as I wrote this book. Tanaya for pitching in and Mona Ma'am and Rohit Sir for giving Myra an extended family. Areeb Khan for once saying I have a sharp learning curve. Here is a book at thirty. Ajay Khullar for challenging me to the race to finish our books. I beat you fair and square. Vishal Gaurav Bana, for timely and crucial insights into school administrative approaches. Rukhsar Saleem for painstakingly transcribing the interviews at a short notice.

Sahir Usman for always being Mr Dependable. You have a heart of gold. Haseeba Mummy and Usman Papa for always being supportive and accommodating. Atiya Rehman and Binish bhabhijaan for loving Myra beyond measure. Maarif bhaijaan for growing up with me and always being my yardstick of excellence. Yasser Usman for being a feminist without clichés. You are the strongest man I know. You are the best man I know. Syed Pervez Jamal, my father, who has always got my back. I love you, Papa. All our stories start with our mothers. Mine does with Shabnam Faridi. Yours is the strength I emulate. I love you, Mamma.

Lastly, the kids: my lovely niece Mishail and my dearest daughter, Myra, may you both grow up together to learn to always love and never hate.

Appendix 1

List of schools

Here's the full list of the schools mentioned in the book. In the asterisked schools the incidents were not reported to the authorities.

The 118 students I spoke to in Delhi NCR, attended the following schools. At least one child in each of these schools reported an incident to me. I reached out to all these schools over email and on the phone to ask if they had had incidents of religious bullying and to get their perspective. Ten schools denied knowledge of such incidents. Only Vasant Valley said they would not comment on a confidential and sensitive matter. Of the remaining schools, Glendale Academy, Manav Rachna, Bal Bharati, Shiv Nadar and DPS Gurgaon said they didn't have knowledge of any such incidents but showed proactive concern on the matter and shared information about regular workshops conducted for children. Of the remaining fourteen schools on this list, nine said they would respond to me if they were interested. None wrote back.

Appendix 1: List of schools

1. Vasant Valley School, Delhi*
2. Sanskriti School, Delhi*
3. Delhi Public School, Mathura Road, Delhi
4. Delhi Public School, Vasant Kunj, Delhi*
5. Delhi Public School, RK Puram, Delhi*
6. Delhi Public School, Noida, Noida*
7. Delhi Public School, Sushant Lok, Gurugram*
8. Delhi Public School, Sector 45, Gurugram*
9. Lotus Valley International School, Noida
10. Mayoor School, Noida
11. Manav Rachna International School, Noida*
12. Bluebells School International, Delhi*
13. Shikshantar, Gurugram*
14. DAV Public School, Sohna Road, Gurugram*
15. Shiv Nadar School, Noida
16. Tagore International School, Delhi*
17. Apeejay School, Noida*
18. Apeejay School, Sheikh Sarai, Delhi*
19. Amity International School, Noida*
20. Bal Bharati Public School, Noida*
21. Laxman Public School, Delhi*
22. Sommerville School, Noida*
23. Glendale Academy, Hyderabad*
24. Daly College, Indore
25. Amtul's Public School, Nainital*

Appendix 2

Excerpts of select interview transcripts

Excerpts from a selection of the interviews conducted across India. Please note that these are only excerpts of interviews that ran into hours at times. These have been included to give the reader a feel of the people who speak in these pages and to include many other voices that were left out.

Interview 1

Email exchange with Azania Safiya Khan, now in college, USA

NE: Hi Azania, your mother shared many incidents from your school in which educated NRI and business-class children study. Would like to hear if you have anything to add about your emotional trajectory when you were going through all this.

Azania: Great to meet you! I am so excited for your book and think this is incredibly important work – more power to you! So much of what is outlined happened to us when we were young… putting young Muslim children on the spot like this (and making them vulnerable to further abuse) would make them even more fearful [of] assert[ing] the validity of their experiences. I remember I had two teachers who were brazenly pro-Modi, my Sanskrit teacher in classes 9 and 10 and my social studies teacher in class 10. She talked about how great Gujarat was and what a good leader Modi is. I raised my hand and said, 'What about 2002?' and she said, 'Modi got rid of the problem-making elements in Gujarat and controlled them.' I was so taken aback by what she said. I didn't really have a response and I know I had tears in my eyes. It really was heartbreaking to see people I know – my friends – nodding their heads in agreement, knowing how visibly upset I was. That really is when I realized being critical of Modi is something often limited to Muslim families. I stopped going to social studies [classes] after that for a while, and I always made excuses like the vice principal had asked to see me, or I was working on a project, or was out of school for debates, etc. I was a school topper in social studies and her attitude towards me after that incident changed drastically. I didn't speak in class after that at all. I felt like my 'repute' as a good student had changed. (She described me as rude and spoiled to another teacher.)

In grades 11 and 12, the school environment was very competitive. I was in the thick of the competition, and seen as a student who was smart academically and intellectually. All teachers seemed pretty fond of me. An entitled, rich classmate with both parents who were senior corporate executives (by the way, both parents are fairly nice people otherwise) would taunt me with statements like:

Is your father okay with you wearing a skirt?

Is your father part of the Taliban? Will he shoot all of us?

Isn't your father angry that your legs are exposed in your skirt? Not that your legs are very shapely (combination of Islamophobia and misogyny).

Don't speak in class. Muslim girls who don't wear a hijab are not allowed to speak.

All this was said in jest. It was supposed to

be humour. Other kids would laugh and I was expected to laugh as well. My not laughing was seen as oversensitivity or not having a sense of humour. This was a particularly difficult period. I do think having the name Azania Khan and fitting into some conventional standard of what Indians find good-looking made me an object of fetishization. I heard lots of comments (and read them online) from upper-caste Hindu boys of how Muslim girls were better-looking than Hindu girls. The way this translated was that I faced a kind of sexualization that I don't think other girls faced, because I was fundamentally an outsider to their social cliques (being Muslim and not being one of the 'family friends' – not part of pujas, arangetrams, weddings, etc., where they all socialized outside of school), so I was on the receiving end of many dehumanizing comments and behaviours. All of my stalkers, whether Punjabi or Tamil, have been upper caste, particularly Brahmin. I think this is relevant because Hinduness was framed as being superior to Islam, and one of the boys was always telling me how Sanskrit is superior to other languages, constantly sending me links to videos and blogs of people like Subramanian Swamy and Rajiv Malhotra. It was seriously weird, as he was doing this *because* he liked me and wanted to prove to me that there was something wrong with me being Muslim. A few other boys who had a crush on me harassed me about being meat-eating and how vegetarianism is more pure and humane (this often came from Marwaris, Jains, etc.). It really felt like they liked me because they wanted to Hinduize me, or at least the focus on me being Muslim was obsessive (particularly on Bakr-Id, they would send me awful videos of goats being killed and say, 'This is what your family does?')

I think one thing (regarding my emotional journey) was that I was made to feel ashamed of my own family and background. I kept trying to prove to people that my parents and grandparents were liberal and progressive, and we weren't a horrid Muslim stereotype. This was against the backdrop of Modi's normalization in the national discourse, so I felt like any comment against me or my family justified violence against Muslims. I was very politically engaged, so I was constantly thinking about how my classmates' 'soft' bigotries were linked to how they would vote in 2014. It really broke me down; I became pretty aggressive as a result. The idea that people who know me and claim to be my friends voted for the BJP still makes me angry, like it's a betrayal.

NE: Thank you for your very open-hearted mail. These are difficult times, and you are a strong girl. Although there is no choice in that matter. One needs to be. These are all stories of our vulnerabilities, strengths and resilience. All the best to you for your path ahead in life. Stay in touch.

Interview 2

With Arshia Shah, Azania's mother

AS: I remember another conversation with a boy from a different school with whom Azania had a debate over politics. This boy was pro-Modi and dismissed all of her data-based arguments with: 'You don't want Modi to win because you are a Muslim. Your argument is not rational. You are overemotional. Your loyalty is not with India's success.' Azania's realization here was that this is not a true debate or discussion, it's a combat.

NE: Even at the school level? This feeling had petered down. It's not limited to Twitter.

AS: It can't be a fact-based discussion any more. It has gone way beyond that. Now we see this tendency in its full-blown form, but Azania says she had begun to see the cracks back in 2013. So although crushes on Muslim girls and Muslim boys were common, no one would ever stand up for Muslim rights or counter the dehumanization of Muslims or labelling them as terrorists or the humour around that. This is Azania's point. My point is that when forty-year-olds don't do it, how can we expect sixteen- to eighteen-year-olds to!

NE: As in?

AS: I always heard stories of discrimination against Muslims, but never having faced any myself I didn't understand it. And then one day I heard a colleague speak at our lunch table of his trip to Mumbai and commenting about a locality he'd passed through: '*Woh bahut gandi locality hai – wahan gande mulle rehte hain* [That's a dirty area – dirty Muslims live there].' A few colleagues who knew [I was Muslim] tried to shut him up.

NE: The other colleagues knew you were a Muslim?

AS: Yes, they did. This particular one didn't as he was new in office and didn't know me that well. A few days later he came and apologized. He said, 'I am sorry I said this in front of you; if I knew you were a Muslim I would not have said it.' I told him that I would have respected him much more if he had said that it was wrong and he shouldn't have said it in the first place. Because saying that it was wrong in front of me meant that you will do it behind my back. Instead best to say that as India is a free country, you are free to say whatever and hate whoever you like and you will do it in front of me. Although he didn't get what I meant, it told me that I don't register as Muslim immediately. But the name I had given to my daughter was very obviously a Muslim one with a Khan in the surname.

NE: Which led to the Paki incident in school.

AS: Yes, and so many more over her growing-up years. So I didn't want this to weigh on her and decided to change her name. In India it is fairly easy to change your name before class 10. So I called her school to find out the procedure and then discussed it with her. I said she could take her father's first name. It wouldn't give away a Muslim identity immediately.

NE: I see, so how did Azania react?

AS: She refused. She said I have grown up with this name and I like it and I will not change it. If it means that I will be discriminated against for my name, I will take it. I could understand where she came from. But as a mother I was apprehensive. When I was in my late twenties, the Bamiyan statues were blown up and as a trained archaeologist I was very pained to see that. And I remember feeling so angry that no one was speaking about it from the community. When the Sikh riots happened in '84, I don't remember a single Muslim standing up and saying it was wrong. We have to learn from other communities on voicing our concern for everyone. If I don't take interest in your life, why the hell will you take interest in mine?

NE: So this subconsciously works against us?

AS: When I was young I remember whenever we were out and there was any congregation of religious men, whether it was mullahs or priests, our mother would hold our hands so much tighter. She would pull us subtly nearer. It was probably subconscious. I remember her telling me of some incident when a maulvi had tried to fondle her brother, so she held the view that all religious men were perverse. And maybe that's why she had a fear of them. And in a crowded place she would hold our hands tight and keep us close. She never said anything but we figured that, OK, she does it only when there are certain kinds of men around. I picked up on the same thing subconsciously and maybe that was why my daughter also picked it from me. As parents we hear and read so much around us, and we pass on our biases to our children in little ways we do not even realize. We had gone to Pakistan when we were young and there was this Hindu family friend who was excited to know about Pakistan on our return. So they asked me how was Pakistan? And I replied at age twelve, 'It was nice, Aunty, but you know there were so many Muslims…there were Muslims everywhere!' [*Laughs*]

NE: Life comes full circle.

Interview 3

With Asma, high school student, Delhi

NE: What is your earliest memory when you realized that the rest of the world is not Muslim?

Asma: When I grew up and started wearing the hijab and everyone started rejecting me. That's when it started hitting me and it made me feel 'Muslim'. In fact, it's from both sides. I remember my friends Priyanka and Karan. I went to their house and had some snacks. Back home my mother reprimanded me, *'Kya khaya … kyun khaya Hindu ke ghar ka?'* That was the time I felt different.

NE: Do you feel guilty for sharing food with your non-Muslim friends?

Asma: Ya, but I do. We all share our tiffins. It's OK I guess. It's a handed-down guilt.

NE: Do you feel love for the religion or fear?

Asma: I certainly don't feel fear.

NE: But not love?

Asma: I do, especially at Moharram time. But other times…

NE: But that was not your first reaction?

Asma: It wasn't. It's just the whole thing around me.

NE: Do you think we are handing down social paranoia to our kids?

Asma: [*Nods vigorously*]

NE: OK, that's a big yes. In what ways do you think you are socially paranoid?

Asma: It's just the way we have to behave. Even though my friends…like the people I am with most of the time…we reject…well not reject totally, but conveniently ignore, the religious side of each other. But when it's me, I feel it's not so.

NE: Give me an instance.

Asma: Like my school friend Zara's family. Most of them are a bit weird about Shia children but Zara is cool. So once she said to me, 'You must watch the Khalifa Omar series' and I was just like…ummm…oh, OK, sure I will watch it.

NE: OK. So how does that contribute to social paranoia?

Asma: It's just like, oh, what if I say the wrong thing at the wrong time? Even with my Hindu friends. It's like…it's like…umm…whenever we are talking about religion I am like constantly checking myself to see if I said anything that can make me very Islamic. If you know what I mean.

Me: Are you on social media?

Asma: Yes.

Me: Is there any anti-Muslim rhetoric there from where you are borrowing this?

Asma: Ya, but for me it's more from people around me. Like this one time one of my friends seriously asked me…she took me aside and said, 'Do you support the ISIS?' and I was like what the hell! That was my first reaction. She was like very serious. Wasn't smiling. She said, 'I am just asking, don't freak out. I am asking you, do you support the ISIS?' I said no! But I wondered, where did that bomb drop from? Why was I being asked this? Did I do something that made her feel so about me? Was there anything in my actions that say I would be OK with killing of people? It confuses you about yourself. I try to understand how they see me.

Me: Did you counter-question?

Asma: I haven't reached the counter-question level. I should. But ISIS and al Qaida are massacring Shias. Why would I support them? There is a distinction. I keep being asked about why I wear the black scarf.

Me: When you hear that, how do you feel?

Asma: Basically just a lot of anger. Inside me. There was frustration for a bit but then…but then I feel numb now. They would randomly call Zara a Taliban or something. Like if you are wearing the hijab they would say, oh, you look like a terrorist. It's just there, it just happens all the time. We are constantly trying to strike a balance between religion, friends…the whole deen and duniya thing. I feel tiny bit scared. Tiny bit rebellious. I am constantly torn between not doing all the things I want to do coz I have to be this good Muslim and then I go to school every single day and there are all these things and I have to act like distancing myself from that identity.

Interview 4

With Sania, IT professional, mother of a ten-year-old, Gurugram

Sania: My kids do not carry a typically Muslim name that you can identify their religion with.

NE: You think it is a convenient name for today's times?

Sania: Oh, obviously, especially in a place like Gurgaon.

NE: So they don't have Muslim family names?

Sania: No, they carry their father's first name as surname. It is common where we belong to.

NE: Where are you from?

Sania: I am from Bareilly. Where are you from?

NE: My parents are from Allahabad. I was born and brought up in Assam. My husband is from

Moradabad. So you can say I am from all over. [*Laughs*]

When was the first time this happened?

Sania: I remember when my daughter was in grade 3 or grade 4 in DPS. And mothers of all kids had a WhatsApp group.

NE: When was this?

Sania: I guess a year and a half or so ago. So basically we were on a WhatsApp group, where we kind of used to discuss classes and kids' issues. Once we had to share our email IDs on the group for a picnic coordination or something. Just after a week of sharing my email ID, my daughter comes to me and says, 'Mum, are you a Pakistani?' And you know, I was taken aback, and I asked her, 'Why did you ask that?'

She said that some boy told her, 'Because you have Khan as surname, it means you are a Pakistani.' I realized that I had given my official email ID, which had Khan as my surname on the WhatsApp group. And I suddenly mentally visualized the conversations that must have led to for one of the kids to come and say that to my lil one. She asked, 'So Mum, what is a Pakistani?'

I reached out to the boy's parents and invited them over. It was a fine boy and fine family otherwise. It was to show them that we are normal too. I thought it best not to talk directly about it.

NE: Do they know what he had said to your daughter?

Sania: No, I don't think so. I didn't put it forward as such, but I presented myself as a mum who would discuss cars and stuff like that with him. So indirectly I tried to put across that we are Muslims, but not the way you think of us. Just get them to get a feel of us beyond the stereotypes. We had a normal conversation. I felt like the mother was a very educated person. It might probably be the exposure kids are getting all the time from the television, on radio. So it might be an influence from multiple sources. One cannot say. I just wanted to invite them and see them, understand them before reaching any conclusion.

NE: Did you report this to the school?

Sania: No, I didn't. I wanted to avoid confrontation.

NE: Was this a one-off case, or was it repeated?

Sania: It was repeated in various other ways. There was another boy who asked her, 'What does Allahabar mean?' I didn't get it. I said, 'What did he say?'

He had said that all Muslims kill and they say Allahabar.

Then I said, 'It is Allah-o-Akbar, which means God is great. And those terrorists who say this, they don't actually believe in it. Anyways I kind of spoke to the kids. And tried demystifying all that's happening around. My kid is ten years old now and talking to other kids. Everyone is questioning kids now, I guess. And it gets me thinking. Like at times, on WhatsApp groups I come across messages which are like that. They are quite radical, at least coming from a mum in a mums' group I find it terrifying at times.

NE: As in?

Sania: Yeah, first time I noticed was around UP elections time and when Yogiji was elected as the CM. The post was so radical in nature. And I wondered, what will she bring up her kids as?

NE: She was a non-Muslim mother, right?

Sania: Yeah, of course.

NE: What do you mean by radical post?

Sania: Well, something – it was an image of a trishul with the words 'It's time to show them the power of trishul'. Who is the 'them' they are talking about? Something on those lines. I don't exactly remember it.

NE: It was shared in the WhatsApp group of the school?

Sania: Yeah.

NE: At that point, she did not know you were a Khan?

Sania: She must have known, or I don't know, or she must not have noticed. Because, Nazia, it happens all the time on Facebook; there are many very good friends of mine and they many times forget and they too do it on FB.

NE: True.

Interview 5

With Rushnae, a first-year college student, Delhi University

NE: You said you were very conscious of your Muslim identity?

Rushnae: Yeah, kind of.

NE: What is your earliest memory of being made conscious or being aware or being reminded or told about it?

Rushnae: Yeah, I remember a very strange thing... There was one kid who was very angry with me that I am a Muslim. He'd say things like, '*Achha yeh toh Mussulman hain* [She is a Muslim].' And he would practically be angry with me. We were very young and I distinctly remember the anger. I was very confused why. But other kids were like, '*Kya farq padta hai agar yeh Mussulman hai toh* [It does not make any difference if she is a Muslim].' But that one kid who got angry with me for being a Muslim, I don't remember his name now, but it left me apprehensive, made me feel something was wrong about me. It stayed with me always.

NE: It was only one kid at that time...some ten years back? What if there are many now who react the same way with a young kid?

Rushnae: It would be very, very disturbing, I guess. Difficult to deal with. Later as we grew up, the difference was more when we became aware of festivals. For Eid, especially, all classmates and friends used to come and specifically greet me. For all other festivals, it used to be like a wish on our WhatsApp group. But for Eid, there was no common wish on any group, but a separate wish directly to me. People will specifically come to wish me Eid Mubarak. Probably not to make it obvious to other people. As if, achha, Eid was only

Rushnae's festival, not for everyone. These were small changes which kept on creeping in, which made me clear about a distinct identity. There were many more such small things that keep adding on. Even if I don't want to, I would feel different.

NE: There were no other Muslim kids with you in class or other batches in your school, Mother's International?

Rushnae: There were…I don't think too many. There was just one set of brothers, senior and junior to me.

NE: So, on an average, every class has one Muslim kid?

Rushnae: Yes, you can say that.

NE: Have you heard of them being called Pakistani?

Rushnae: No, I don't think…it never happened in my class or with those brothers. But there were common jokes like those jokes on Sardars.

NE: For Muslim kids?

Rushnae: For them it was like, 'Don't piss them off, they will bomb you.' Though it never looked so vicious when it happened one or two times. But over time they would. Jokes used to be, like, taken lightly.

NE: They used to be in the same vein as the Sardar jokes. But tell me more about the jokes.

Rushnae: Oh, it used to be very low-key. Many times what happens is that you too take it for granted if you are the only one. What else to do?

Mother interjects: As a parent I have to say I didn't know this.

Rushnae: Haan, coz it was pretty low-key. Repetitive, but low-key. It's just always there. Post–May 2014 school became extremely weird. It wasn't like a very traumatic experience. But it became very strange. I was in senior school and there was a lot of discussion on everything that was happening in the country. It became awkward discussing current affairs. Most of the people started behaving as if everything was like an OK thing or no big deal. And I used to enter the conversations and they would either trail off or ask me about my views on Gujarat. They used to say to me, why do you care so much about the riots? 'It was just one little riot. How does it affect you?' So these things started happening. That's when I became very strongly like…OK I am a Muslim. And I used to get very angry, not with what had happened, but what bothered me was people did not actually care about what and how things are happening to people like me. At that point I thought only Muslims were being targeted; now I know it's many others like Dalits and other marginalized [sections]. But then it used to be like Muslims are targeted and nobody just seems to care. So I was like, why should I not completely embrace being a Muslim? Maybe just start wearing a hijab.

NE: Still, I don't follow, why would you want to do that?

Rushnae: No, the thing is, I was just angry,

basically. That no one even bothered to think about what kind of person was coming to power and what it means for many Indians. They couldn't see beyond the rhetoric he put out and things started becoming communalized in class. It was like everyone was talking like this, from classmates to teachers. And then later crazy things started happening. There was one teacher who was from Jasola, and when Delhi elections happened she was like my constituency is a Muslim constituency; it's a criminal constituency, so Kejriwal is bound to win.

NE: And this happened in front of you?

Rushnae: Yes.

NE: She knew that you are a Muslim?

Rushnae: Yes, she knew. As I said, people suddenly simply did not care that some will be very badly affected by such words. There was an economics teacher also. And there was one tuition teacher also.

NE: So, describe them.

Rushnae: So, basically, I was at my tuition class and there was this kid who got some sweets. So the teacher says, 'I will get some spoons. Don't start eating like this; don't eat like Muslims.' And I was like, WHAT? And she said, 'Oh, they are dirty na; they eat badly na.' I said, 'No ma'am, nothing like that happens in my family; no one eats like animals.' Then she said, 'Ohhhh achha, but I was not talking about you; I was talking about the uneducated people.' She kind of got very apologetic about it. But I felt like she can't take back what she just said.

NE: So, when you decided to take on the hijab?

Rushnae: My family was never very practising Muslims per se. But the connection was there culturally. I didn't think myself too much of a Muslim before. But when these things started happening I just got very angry. I just decided I am gonna do it. Wear a hijab now. Coz anyway people are not going to trust me. They would ask, 'You don't look like a Muslim, you don't wear a hijab.'

NE: Why?

Rushnae: It is more like an expression of anger. I might as well do it. Coz people are going to see you as that only so might as well be more closely associated with it. Wear the identity. It's like, I think you are part of a cosmopolitan culture… like no one cares if you are Muslim or not, like myself…but then you realize you are not. You realize you are the other and people will not accept you completely ever. So might as well just be completely Muslim so that you have somewhere to go back to. Otherwise you end up nowhere. Neither a Muslim nor [part of] an emancipated community; you have nothing. If these people I grew up with in school are not accepting me completely, then I just as well might be what they think I am.

NE: Do you still believe that?

Rushnae: No, not really. Now I have become less angry. Once I went to a good college. And there I met a lot of people who are more aware or simply do not care about these things. So in a way it was a good change. And in college I have seen a lot more Muslim people. And for the first time in my life, I made friends who are Muslims and who were not from my family or related to me.

NE: So now you have friends who are Muslims. Interesting.

Rushnae: These were the people I did not meet through family. I met them independently.

NE: So you were friends with them only because they were Muslims?

Rushnae: No, they were in my class. And we actually were among the very few people who attended class. We got closer because of that.

NE: How many Muslims are there in college?

Rushnae: I can't really count. But in my class there are a few. And they are all not the stereotypes I myself had started to expect from Muslims. They are all normal people. I am also not a major example any more. There are others also. Now I know more Muslim people than I knew before. And I am around with more people, not those I met through family. So it is such a relief to know people on your own. In school the world was smaller and scarier.

NE: Now you feel the spotlight has moved away from you?

Rushnae: No, now it is like I am not the only one about whom they feel, how come Muslims are so progressive? But now there are other people also who are like that. There is no specific me… *Arre bhai yeh kaise?* [Oh, how come she is like this?]

NE: Do you think it made you feel odd?

Rushnae: No, I would say I used to feel more conscious.

NE: You were comfortable in being conscious?

Rushnae: Oh, not at all. It was a very uncomfortable consciousness.

Interview 6

With Zuveria, mother of a ten-year-old, Hyderabad

NE: When was the first time your kids realized that the rest of the world is not Muslim? Because growing up we tend to believe the world is as our homes are.

Zuveria: Surprisingly, they learnt this fact in school only. Especially, very...I would say…very openly…after Modi became PM. As kind of everybody knew that Muslim sentiment was not towards Modi for what Modi had done in the past. Especially for my son. I guess he was then in first grade… One of his classmates comes and says to him, 'You are a Muslim. You should go to Pakistan.'

NE: In Hyderabad?

Zuveria: Yes, in Hyderabad.

NE: In which school?

Zuveria: Glendale.

NE: OK, that's surprising. As it's a Muslim-run institution.

Zuveria: Yes, it's a Muslim-run institution, but they don't have any biases for Muslims in particular. It's pretty fair. And one of the most respected schools in Hyderabad. This was happening in classes between the kids. So it was for the first time my boy got a feeling like that in Hyderabad.

NE: And how did your child react?

Zuveria: He wasn't able to understand. He was like why was he asking me to go to Pakistan. I live here.

NE: Right. So what did you say when your child came to you with this?

Zuveria: I was like…[*pauses to think*]…I told him that we made the choice of who wants to go to Pakistan way back. Now we live in Hyderabad. And I was like religion has got nothing to do with where you live. In fact, religion teaches you to stay loyal to your land.

NE: So he came back to you and told you that this happened?

Zuveria: Yeah. He was pretty disturbed that somebody has asked him to leave India and go… [*Laughs hesitantly*]

NE: How did you all react to this?

Zuveria: They all had undergone that same thing during that phase. All three of my kids had gone through it.

NE: So it was like somebody who had come to power and then things changed?

Zuveria: I don't think my kids knew about the Gujarat riots. We had to explain all this is why we don't prefer Modi. As this is what he had done.

NE: So coming back, what do you think, as a Muslim mother, are the elements that you are handing down to your child? What does it mean to them to be Muslim? What makes them Muslim?

Zuveria: Their behaviour, the way they think, the humanity side of the religion. Because I tell them it's important for you to pray, fast, read the Quran and everything. But you have to be human first. Islam, the religion, that's between you and God. But how you prove to the world that you are a Muslim is how you treat people around you irrespective of their religion, caste, class.

Interview 7

With Seema, a student in high school, Mumbai

Seema: So, I was in class 4 or 5; I still remember where we were rehearsing for a play near nursery block, something happened and somebody said something about being Muslim. I just said, 'I am a Muslim too,' and everyone just started looking and gaping at me. And everybody was like, 'You don't look like one!'

NE: How old were you then?

Seema: I was nine or ten. I remember this clearly as I had fallen down from the stage. That's how I remember, about discrimination. Other people who are not Muslim, they don't understand you. They probably think you are a crocodile or something. That time I realized how it feels to be different.

NE: How did you realize you are different?

Seema: Aaaaa...I didn't actually. It just happened one after the other...like someone had come to school, who was a cricketer. And I was in class 7 or 8, and I was with a friend and I really liked that guy. So my friend said, you don't even tell people in your family. They will come with knives and stuff. I was told, *Tumhare yahan toh bahut honge aise log jo chaku-chhuri chalate hain?* [You must surely have knife-wielding members in your family?] And I was taken aback at this perception of my family. I had no idea where that came from.

NE: So your friends thought your family to be...?

Seema: Yeah, my best friends were sort of growing up. We all dressed up same. We spoke the same way. My dresses used to be as short as their dresses used to be and my parents too were equally cool about everything. I used to look 'normal' in every way. I did not have those scary parents. I wasn't different from them in any way. But I was so different for them in many ways.

NE: Because you were Muslim?

Seema: Yeah, because I was Muslim.

NE: That was the only differentiating point?

Seema: No, it was not a contradiction. I was *not* different, but *that* made me different. Do you understand how it used to make me feel? One time my friend took me aside and very seriously asked me, 'Do you support al-Qaeda?' It was like a bomb dropped on me. I said *no*! I didn't counter question because she asked so sweetly. So I find myself constantly checking on what I say and what I do not say about religion.

Mother interjects: There is always the 'you don't look like a Muslim' standard line that we all face. A friend from college in Miranda House, Delhi University, said to me, 'You don't look like a Muslim!'

So I asked her, 'What is a Muslim supposed to look like?' And my friend said, 'Well you know… but you are so pretty!'

'So?'

'I mean you don't wear kajal, neither is your nose pierced. And you have short hair!'

'And how many Muslims do you know personally?

'Oh so many! My meat-wala is Muslim and my neighbourhood masterji is Muslim.'

'And are they supposed to be connected to me in any way for me to look like them? Or are all Muslims supposed to be like that?'

'Ah-oh.'

Interview 8

With Alia, mother of a ten-year-old, Jasola, Delhi

NE: So, in South Delhi all kids are used to being called Paki?

Alia: I believe all Muslim kids from South Delhi at some point must have been called Paki. It's a possibility.

NE: And how do you know all?

Alia: Because at least who all I know, I have met, have been called Paki. In a way, yes, it is a generalization. But I strongly suspect it.

NE: For example, people you know?

Alia: All of us, like, who are going from Okhla to various schools, we all have experienced at some point or the other.

NE: Like your immediate family or neighbours or what?

Alia: We always have heard so in school. Only difference is that our parents used to say, 'It's not a problem, it all happens, do understand.' But when it happened with my son, I kicked up a fuss about it.

NE: Tell me your memory about it.

Alia: For me, it had happened just once. And it happened too late.

NE: Your school was in central Delhi?

Alia: No, it was in South Delhi.

NE: Which school was this?

Alia: It was Tiny Tots earlier and later it was Sardar Patel. Both are in South Delhi, one is in Greater Kailash, the other is in Lodhi Estate.

NE: OK.

Alia: By the time it happened with me, I was old enough to take care of it myself.

NE: You were in which class?

Alia: I think it was class 9…or 10…either of the two. For my younger sister, it had happened earlier. She was much younger. So she changed schools, and in that particular school, there were a lot of children from refugee families in East of Kailash. So she was very upset.

NE: What exactly had happened with you?

Alia: I just have this memory, someone had called me. I don't know who. I mean I don't remember the person now. My thing had happened [when] I was in Sardar Patel, which was a Gujarati school. Babri Masjid had just been abolished. So sentiment was strong then. But it was post that, I remember.

NE: And you were called a Paki? How did you react?

Alia: Yeah, I had told the pol. science teacher. Because I had joined the school a few days back only. I remember she breathed fire into the classroom and took care of everything.

NE: And you came back and told your parents?

Alia: Yeah.

NE: How did they react?

Alia: Theirs was usual. It was: 'People do such things; we have to listen. Listening to them does not make us Pakistani; we are Indians only.' And they used to say, 'We were the ones who decided to stay back. So if someone is calling you a Pakistani, you do not become a Pakistani.'

NE: You said your sister was very young?

Alia: Yeah, she was very young and more disturbed by it.

NE: Because she did not understand the entire Partition angst?

Alia: No, I think the angst was just that how can you call me a Pakistani, when I am an Indian?

NE: When Abir faced the same thing, how was your reaction – different from or same as your parents'? And why?

Alia: I think that how one deals with these issues

is also different from my parents' generation and mine.

NE: How was it different?

Alia: I will…protest for my rights, they wouldn't.

NE: Why do you think so?

Alia: Different kind of exposure. And also I think the kind of education that they had been given. One has become more assertive than they were. In the sense that I will be ready to take it up and fight it.

NE: Because you believe we have rights enshrined in the Constitution?

Alia: I guess they were more trained into being under the thumb of authority. I don't know.

NE: Even I am trying to understand why they were not. My parents were also not assertive. What makes us more assertive and aware about being wronged?

Alia: No, I think awareness about being wronged was there. But the thing to say that we have been wronged was not there. The sense of being wronged was there. The sense that you can actually make it a point to create a fuss about it was not there.

NE: Does it get influenced by the larger conversation?

Alia: Yes, and I would also say that [there is a] certain class of people who can. I mean, you can, I can. I won't say every person who has been wronged would be able to do that. We can do that because my education lets me do that. Not everyone can. It is a class issue as well.

NE: What did you say to your son, when you heard the same being repeated with him? What was your first reaction when he told you? In which class was he then?

Alia: I think third grade. I am trying to recall. He was upset. There was something happening at that time. I don't remember. It was in the midst of some conflict…what happened two years back, some major political event?

NE: Aam Aadmi Party had come to power in Delhi?

Alia: No, it was something Indo-Pak only. It was around something that some child had said to him, '*Arre, tum to Pakistani ho* [Oh, you are a Pakistani].'

NE: I think a cricket match?

Alia: Maybe a cricket match.

NE: But how did he come and tell you?

Alia: Yeah, he does tell me everything, what happened to him all through the day. So it was part of that.

NE: How did you phrase it?

Alia: I remember that he was very angry. So part of the counselling was it is all right to be a Pakistani but you are not a Pakistani.

NE: OK, interesting.

Alia: Because we have conversations with him. So he understood. At one level, he dealt with it.

NE: Do you feel now that he can handle such situations on his own?

Alia: I think it's a continuous process where he might have been able to handle it on his own. That time, things and events around him…you know, exposure changes…then a kind of readiness develops that you always have. It happens when something happens continuously.

NE: How is his relation with his Indian identity?

Alia: I think he stands up for his national anthem!

Interview 9

With Ranu Bhogal, teacher at a DPS branch in Delhi

RB: Recently we decided to reshuffle the children. Two parents from a section came and said, 'We want our child to be shifted; there is too much of "M factor" in this class.' Those are exactly the words [that were] used. And they were obliged.

NE: This was done last year?

RB: No, this time. This session only, when we started in April 2017. The moment we made the sections in April, that day only they came and felt that there are too many Muslim students. So they wrote against it.

NE: So these were non-Muslim parents?

RB: They were Punjabis.

NE: So these were the parents whose kids were studying French?

RB: No, their kids were not studying French. When the sections were made and parents must have seen the list, they must have decided then.

NE: How do parents get the list?

RB: I don't know. Maybe through WhatsApp

groups. We make groups for parents in which they mention their child's name. I don't know how exactly, but there are a few parents who always have access to all the things. So they wrote a letter. Therefore, the section of these two–three children was switched.

NE: This was the reason given? That there were too many Muslim children in that particular section?

RB: Yes, this is the language they use: M factor. We came to know later that this was why the school agreed to sections being switched. So we objected that if we do this for one kid, then naturally we'll have five more applications. We had this problem but they obliged.

NE: OK. So any instance where teachers have also showed such attitude when sections were getting shuffled?

RB: No, they keep mentioning, not specifically and openly. But there are a few very good teachers who have this thing and mention the M factor. Very educated teachers but they always keep referring to 'M's'. This is always how they speak. They don't take names. Naturally, they were talking about some behaviour issues. They are referring to the EWS children, mostly who are Muslims in our school. And they had some behavioural issues, which teachers had generalized as M factor.

Like there is a child in my class in class 4. And the counsellor knew about this child since class 2. And from the very first day the counsellor came and told me to be very careful about this child as the father is a butcher and mother is not educated and there is nobody at home to take care of him. And most probably he has been abused as he has come to the school with injuries. When the counsellor spoke to him, he just refused to respond.

NE: What is the generalization of the teacher?

RB: Even if the child is good, they feel biased towards the Muslim-class sections, means there is something wrong in understanding. I had two Muslim children in my class from EWS, and both are scholars. I awarded both of them; I gave a book to one of them because she is a driver's daughter and is excellent in everything, and the other one is also very good. But teachers publicly keep saying, 'There are too many Muslims.'

NE: Any particular instance where any scholar child suffered because of the larger generalization?

RB: No, not possible. Even if they feel, they can't generally [do anything] as everything is recorded or marked. So they can't penalize a child just like that. Attitude difference, yes. There are some who have this problem.

NE: What about between children? Have you heard of anything about them?

RB: Yes, they are extremely aggressive. Like there was a child in my class in class 3. She kept saying wrong things. It's both ways. She kept on saying something wrong. So I called her and said, 'What is wrong with you?' She said my mother has asked me not to speak to them as they keep on abusing our religion. So, don't speak to them.

NE: This was a Muslim child?

RB: No, this was a Hindu child. She told me her mother has asked her not to talk to them and they are very bad. This has also happened especially with tiffin.

NE: Was there any instance when the matter escalated to the admin?

RB: Yes, there was a mother who reported that her child refuses to come to school. Her child had told her that kids in school keep telling him that he is a Muslim. And he has become very quiet now. So then they tend to get aggressive, this is also there. And this leads to their difficult behaviour.

NE: How early or in which class do these incidents start getting reported – about being called names, which implies such aggressive behaviour? Or which was the earliest class when you got to know about it? Do these incidents ever get reported to the admin?

RB: No, this is something teachers can handle. Generally, these complaints come to the class teacher and she handles all this very well.

NE: How frequently is it reported to the class teacher?

RB: Again, it depends on the teacher. Like from day one, I am very secular and in my talk also. So I don't get so many complaints and at the end of the year I feel my children are very open to other religions.

There are some children who said a child did not fold hands during the prayer. So I told the child it is perfectly normal, it is up to you. We have all the prayers in English and Hindi, and Gayatri Mantra. We tell the children to pray the way they want. The only thing I tell children is to connect on your own, just by speaking you do not connect with god. Important part is to connect, speaking those lines is not the only thing.

NE: Coming back to my question, how often do these incidents get reported?

RB: It is generally at least three–four times in a year.

NE: How do you tell them that their mother is wrong?

RB: We don't tell [them] your mother is wrong. I try to tell them a story or something like that.

NE: How do you react to parents in such cases?

RB: Once a mother asked me to change the place of her child. I kept counselling them. She tried to convince me that her child does not want to sit in that side of the class.

NE: So earliest was class 3, when you heard of such instances?

RB: No, I have heard it even in classes 1 and 2. It is very common in early age. In classes 1 and 2, kids know about their identity and of other kids being Muslims.

NE: So, you have not heard about senior classes?

RB: Generally, no. Teachers do say there is a lot of disturbance behaviour-wise as there are a lot of Muslim students. By Muslims they imply EWS kids more. And to some extent behavioural issues are there as there is very little monitoring by their parents at home. Generally, mothers are house helps, so they are not at home most of the time.

NE: Do you have some Muslim students who are not in the EWS category?

RB: Yes, very few.

NE: So when you say there are Muslim students from upper-class and EWS categories, do you see the same behaviour among them?

RB: Behaviour-wise, no. Attitude-wise also, no… they are not very similar.

NE: What happens when these incidents are escalated to the admin? What is their usual stand? How do they react to such issues?

RB: No, it does not get escalated to that level. It gets sorted out by teachers only.

NE: How long have you been working in this school?

RB: Twelve years now.

NE: Have you noticed any difference in attitude over a period of time? What kind of changes specifically?

RB: Yes, over a period of time, changes have come. Now parents are concerned about which section their child is in.

NE: Muslim parents also are concerned similarly?

RB: No, generally Muslim students are in EWS. They are not concerned about it at all. But they are always concerned about the treatment their children get.

NE: So, in the last twelve years, what kind of difference has come in teachers and students? What do you have to say about it if different sections get created along religious lines, what is the consequence?

RB: Many teachers opt only for sections that don't have Muslims.

NE: What about you?

RB: No, I have always been given sections which have Urdu students, G and H.

Interview 10

With Sumira, mother of two toddlers, Noida

Sumira: We used to read *Qul a'uudhi bi rabbin naas*, and after reading it we'd become fearless like the lion while passing the ground [*Giggles nostalgically*].

NE: How many girls used to read this with you?

Sumira: We were three friends – Richa Agarwal, Prachi Rawat and me.

NE: Did they know that they were reciting Arabic verses? How old were you then?

Sumira: I guess...we were in fifth or sixth standard, or a little younger. Maximum we must have been below ten years. So what actually used to happen – while crossing that ground [in boarding school campus], they used to get scared. So I too started getting scared seeing them. And when I went home for the holidays I told my abba about this fear. He told me to recite this Arabic verse.

NE: Your friends never asked what you were making them recite?

Sumira: [*After a pause*] We were too small to think or judge anyone or the verse. They just took everything at face value as I was their friend. So they simply trusted me.

I think those times were different. Earlier people were not so judgemental of anyone's practices or choices. But now people will be quite judgemental of you.

NE: So how long did it keep happening?

Sumira: [*Laughs*] For quite a while. And when they went home for the holidays they must have told their families. Then their family probably made them learn the Hanuman Chalisa to counter fear.

NE: So how did the transition happen, from reciting an Arabic verse to the Hanuman Chalisa?

Did you notice any difference? Was there a sudden awareness of difference in religion in them?

Sumira: No, I don't think so. For a couple of years, we went on reciting the Arabic verse only. It was after a few years, some conversation must have happened in their families and they would have made them learn. So later they started reciting Hanuman Chalisa, probably thinking that this is their thing to recite to combat fear. [*Pauses*] Or probably they may have been taught Hanuman Chalisa normally at home. And with time they figured out what is their own thing to recite to combat fear. At the end of the day, both worked. When I was in school, a temple construction was going on.

NE: Inside the school?

Sumira: No, there was a society beside the school. Inside that society temple construction was going on. And our school playground was at some distance from the site of construction. At times we used to go from the playground into that area, where construction was going on.

On the entrance, a few shlokas were written: *Om bhūr bhuvaḥ svaḥa*... I remember very clearly those verses as I used to go there and read them all the time.

So it is like when you are a kid, you do not know all these things that we can't go there or can't wear this. But slowly while growing up these differences start creeping in.

NE: Right.

Sumira: Once curfew was clamped in the city due to some riots and schools were shut, but we were in the hostel. So classes were not happening and we were sitting on our beds inside the hostel. There was a cleaner, who while sweeping the floor was telling our matron about the incident which led to the riots.

As he was sweeping the floor in the outer portion of the hostel, I heard him say, 'They cut them into pieces and threw the bodies into the drain.'

And then I realized that it's the Muslims who have done so. Then a realization dawned on me that I am a Muslim here. And how Muslims in the city have murdered Hindus. He was sharing chilling details with the matron about how Hindus were blocked from both the sides, were murdered and thrown in the drain which was in that area. That grotesque picture which he was describing was making me increasingly fearsome about the fact that I am a Muslim here. And I was in eighth standard [at] that time.

NE: Class 8 means you must have been thirteen or fourteen.

Sumira: [*With a gasp*] That was one time I realized I am different, that is, a Muslim here.

NE: And a fourteen-year-old being quite aware as a female.

Sumira: I was feeling I am a Muslim and there he was saying what Muslims had done. So you get a feeling in your heart and you think in that manner. It was a distinct moment of realization of my identity. On the other hand, the Muslim boys who were there in school, I was never good friends with them – my friends were different. But I remember talking to those Muslim boys and discussing amongst each other, in case something happens to us being Muslims, how are we going to run away from here?

NE: As fourteen-year-olds.

Sumira: We, Muslim kids, how will we run away from here? So one suggested we should run along the railway track, which was close to the school.

NE: This is your classmate telling you?

Sumira: No, all Muslim students together were discussing and deciding.

NE: Where were you sitting when you had this discussion?

Sumira: We had met during the playtime in the evening in our hostel.

NE: All of these are hostellers?

Sumira: Yes, only hostellers were stuck inside the hostel due to curfew outside. I had heard about this incident of killings in the daytime. So in the evening we [Muslim students] had gathered to talk. We were five or six of us.

NE: Had Muslim students ever come together before?

Sumira: No, never. Muslims students in school had never come together.

NE: How did you all come together?

Sumira: We just went and talked to each other. As we thought that we had to speak to each other.

NE: So how did it start? Two students met and spoke to each other, and then the third joined in? So all of them were feeling scared?

Sumira: We kind of felt an affinity to talk to each other as we felt if people started hitting/killing us, then what we will do? How will we run from here? Eventually, we decided we would run along the railway track.

NE: And this is all fourteen-year-olds making a plan?

Sumira: This was decided so as to save ourselves if something happens to us. It is best to escape by running from here if someone catches us or tries to harm us. I was so scared there, thinking how and what they all must be thinking about me as I was a Muslim girl among them. I used to feel that everyone is looking at me.

NE: You were feeling all were looking at you?

Sumira: Yes, they must be judging me, looking at me as a few Muslims have killed Hindus. That was scary. I felt all eyes constantly on me. That was the point when differences that had begun to grow between us kids were marked out for life, laced with fear.

Interview 11

With Saira Shah Halim, daughter of an army war veteran who last served as the deputy chief of army staff, Indian Army

SSH: It was my roommate in college who asked me, '*India–Pakistan ka match hota hai toh tum kisko cheer karti ho?* [Who do you cheer for in an India–Pakistan match?]'

NE: Did she know you were an army kid?

SSH: Yes. I said to her, 'You must be ashamed as you too are from the defence forces, a BSF officer's daughter. My father is a '71 war veteran of the Indian national army. Isn't it quite apparent who we cheer for?'

NE: How did she respond?

SSH: She had put it so casually and wasn't confrontational.

NE: Yes, asking Indian Muslims, be it civilians or from the army, whether or not they support

Pakistan is very mundane. Casual. Everybody's birthright perhaps.

Interview 12

With Humaira, a young lawyer in Bhopal

Humaira: I remember witnessing a brawl that broke out in court when I was working in Mumbai. It had involved one of the clients of my firm. He was incidentally a Muslim and I had been overseeing his case. Later in our chambers the team was laughing and we were making fun of the 'cartoons' that we often seemed to have to represent. Suddenly one of my colleagues sitting with me says seriously, '*Arre, tumhare religion mein sab aise hi baat karte hain na...gaali aur maar-peet se?* [People from your religion talk like this, right? With curses and physical abuse.]' I was shocked and asked him if he had ever seen me speak with disrespect. He said, 'But you are different.'

NE: Yes, we don't let go of stereotypes in spite of education. It only gets strengthened with time.

Humaira: When I was very young, maybe six or

seven, I used to keep hearing about Osama bin Laden and the wars that would keep happening. And I started saying, 'Amma, I wanna be a terrorist.' My mom was justly horrified and said, 'Beta, are you insane? Just because you are angry and you keep hearing about it doesn't make you a terrorist.' Fortunately I had parents who were much aware of this nonsense. In school all I would hear about was how all Muslims are terrorists. And when you ask them if I look like a terrorist, then they say, 'No, you are not, but you know others are.' The pictures of riots and victims are seen by young children and it keeps playing in your mind again and again. With awareness of having been singled out – in so many ways – lynching, love jihad. Things keep happening to you in today's India.

Interview 13

With Sabina, IT professional and mother of two teenagers, Noida

Sabina: My younger son came to me as I was packing and said, 'Mama, please, do you really need to wear this for the holiday?' He pointed towards my hijab. Astounded by his words, I left the packing and holiday planning discussion midway. I asked as I hugged him tight, 'Why do you say that, sweetheart?' He said, 'There was this family who was pulled off the plane for wearing a hijab... They will send you away too and I will be left alone.'

NE: Was he referring to that incident – sometime back there was a spate of such aeroplane deportations?

Sabina: Yes, I couldn't hold back my tears. I had to console him but it was just so choking. I said, 'No, sweetheart, no one except Allah can take me away from you.' But he was persistent, 'But if they take you away from me…what will I do?' It was one of those moments when one starts thinking about what I am doing and why.

NE: Don't the kids often ask you why you wear a hijab? No one else in your family does.

Sabina: Recently when I came back from hajj, I was wearing the customary headscarf. And then I simply kept it on. It felt weird to remove it after having worn it for almost a month for the pilgrimage. I wore it much to the surprise of everyone in my family and colleagues. But slowly they got used to it. I believe good parenting is also a form of ibaadat [worship]. So I try to simplify concepts by giving them an example of a video game they play. As there are different levels in the video game. Life is pretty much similar. You are moving from one level to another and there are different challenges. Everyone is at a different level. And everyone has a different approach and strategy for the game. You collect rewards as you go. The highest level is Jannat. You have to aim for that. There is no money there. You have to earn points through good deeds to use as your currency to spend in Jannat. So when the younger one who is always competing doesn't listen, I tell him that the elder one will get a Lamborghini and he will get a Maruti Alto in Jannat. So the younger one quickly follows to the washroom to wash up for his namaz. [*Laughs*] So I tell them this is one of my ways to earn for Jannat.

NE: They understand?

Sabina: Sometimes they do. But mostly it's people around me outside that don't understand. It makes going for corporate presentations difficult. So slowly I have transitioned to a more inward-looking role in my start-up.

NE: It's interesting to reflect on how many independent women take up the hijab of their own accord. For some it's a place for comfort, for some it's an identity, for some it gives security, for many others it's the word of God. There are as many reasons as there are colours of the hijab. I wish the explanation for it was as homogeneous as the perception of it is.

Interview 14

With Maryam, young development professional, Hyderabad

Maryam: I remember the first time I decided to start wearing the hijab. I was wearing it and had stood as a volunteer at a programme and suddenly, for the first time, I felt my identity as a Muslim.

NE: It was a marker, of course.

Maryam: Yes, but I had not thought of it like that till then. Suddenly, I felt too many eyes on me. I was uncomfortable with the distinction. Though now I have come to terms with it. Over time I have had such weird questions thrown at me for my hijab that I used humour to make up for it. My friends in college would keep asking me if I wore my scarf while bathing too. I [would] say, 'Yes! I have a shampoo called Scarves and Shoulders.' It is only five seconds later that they go OHH!

I got married recently, and when my friend Aditi came home a few days ago, she said, 'It's so nice to come to your house, yaar, it doesn't feel like I have come to a Muslim house.'

So you see, people have stereotypes. Every class has one to three Muslims. How many can they befriend in a class of sixty? So the majority of kids are still growing up without a Muslim friend. Even those who do, have stereotypes deeply ingrained. I shudder to think what those who do not have a Muslim in their friends circle think of us! I have a childhood friend, Preeta, who used to come to my house regularly. But when we grew up and got married, she came to my place and met my husband and his multicultural friends. She later remarked, 'Your hubby is so cosmopolitan, *kitne* broad-minded *hain*...' I asked her, 'What about you and me?' She said, '*Arre haan!*' She found my husband's non-Muslim friends odd but not the friendship she and I shared. So I realized somewhere down the line even she has been fed at some level.

Interview 14

With Ayesha Bilgrami, retired advertising professional, Bengaluru

NE: With everything that is happening is there a social anxiety you feel ingrained in the kids?

AB: I am sure there is. I am quite sure there is. It's natural but also scary because that social anxiety only creates affinities and then you hang out with certain people. It is like people living in ghettos also, where you feel safer with a certain crowd. Then you are meeting those people more. I mean you seek out your comfort level.

We did not have that anxiety ourselves as we were multicultural. You know, we had friends from all over, Hindu, Muslim, Sikh, Jain... Because we were very secure in our space. We didn't feel threatened. But that is changing in the present generation.

NE: But the social anxiety is there now in you too?

AB: Not for me, it's not. Because today I am not bothered. Even if I don't have friends and if I meet two people even at this age of mine that is still anyway enough.

NE: Worried about your child?

AB: I don't see it in him right now. But I will not be surprised if it changes. I [mean] generally, if I were to say, his children will face it. Because there is an anxiety when you feel you can't be open or normal or stay in a natural way or express yourself or have no freedom to say what you wish without being dubbed as anti-national or anti-this or anti-that.

NE: Have you had the experience of wearing nationalism on your sleeve when you were outside?

AB: Yes, I had heated arguments over it. And I had an argument only recently on this demonetization issue. When I had my dear friends telling me that you are against it because you are anti-government. I told them I have never heard such bull crap in my life. Is criticizing what your elected government does…is that going to make you anti-government? Yes, I have been anti-government from day one… whether it was Indira Gandhi, Narasimha Rao, Vajpayee on various issues…! After all, we are electing them. If we can elect them…then we can criticize them.

NE: Now everything ends at soldiers?

AB: Yeah, now if we criticize them, then we are anti-government, it is ridiculous. Whatever I am, I am. I will continue being like this. Tomorrow it might be some other person, if he/she does something which is not right, I will criticize it too. See, it's my privilege to say that.

See, people like me can put a point across forcefully, hold my ground; it doesn't affect my job, it doesn't affect my children's admission in school, it doesn't affect my getting a house on rent now.

All those are over and done for me now.

NE: Right!

AB: If I were twenty years younger, I would have been worried whether my child will get admission or not, if I am searching for an apartment whether I will get it or not, what people will say to me at my job, then I am under pressure. Immense pressure to conform, to shut up, to not be seen for who I am.

Interview 16

With Rakhshanda Jalil, mother of two girls, New Delhi

RJ: '*Muslims terrorist hote hain. Muslims nahate nahin hain, Muslims gande hote hain…bahut shaadiyan karte hain…* [Muslims are terrorists, Muslims don't bathe, Muslims are dirty…they marry several times…]' We all have heard this all our lives. So I was leaving work early at IHC [India Habitat Centre] as I was getting engaged and I informed my boss, and she says, 'But Muslim men make very bad husbands!' For a woman in her fifties to say this to a young woman about to get engaged was bizarre. Another dear friend's father sits me down and, [looking] very concerned, says, 'What guarantee do you have that he will not marry again?' I said, 'What guarantee does anyone have for anything in life? What if I fall in love with someone else?' These were all good people. But they asked such things.

Delhi University is a melting pot. You have all classes coming there and sharing classrooms, canteen and metro. For many of them it's the first exposure to a girl. In my daughter's first year she would share how boys would walk up to her and try to randomly pick her up. The class difference was glaringly visible and that water got further muddied by religion. She stopped using her real name in fact. It becomes a *kya samajhti hai yeh Mussulman apne aap ko?* [what does this Muslim think of herself?]

NE: Is that what she said to you?

RJ: It's the sense one gets as a parent picking up from kids' words and hesitations. I remember I took up work in the Jamia Millia University and we shifted close to the campus from Gulmohar

Park. In Jamia my daughter could not simply pick up the phone and order a pizza. Like she was used to. In Delhi you don't just change an address and a landline number but change one way of life for another when you move from Gulmohar Park to Jamia. For my daughter's first birthday in Jamia the attendance dropped sharply. Gulmohar Park was a hep neighbourhood and everybody wanted to come. But in Jamia they would say, '*Uss taraf ka idea nahin hain* [Don't have any idea about that area].'

Communal bias is built into our minds and usually we take it for granted but every now and then it becomes very sharp. Things like Batla House encounter or something like that. For this the whole neighbourhood got branded, though Batla House was very far. From service providers to dry-cleaners to florists, all services got affected. We became branded as people not deserving of these basic services.

Differences in India are actually not along the lines of religion but class. Differences can also be provincial or big city. But it's an artificial divide we are creating that politics and media is further playing on. We all have multiple identities...we are

Indians, we are North Indians; within that there is region, there is caste… We think that being Indian Muslims we are burdening our children with consciousness of self. But if you look around there are others with even more issues. And others are even more niche. You can turn it into a joke and look inward and rejoice in who you are. Own up and revel in it. It's just another layer of identity. Burden would be when I am labouring under it. It's there in my consciousness. But not a burden. It's other people's problem that they see me only as a Muslim. They will strike up a conversation with me and talk of Urdu. How sweet it is. I say sure, so what? They don't expect my opinion on anything else.

NE: There was a feeling of being 'different'?

RJ: This thing happened with us also. But in the field of education. Abbu [father] and Maami [mother] gave us this impression casually, not through a proper sit-down or proper chat, just a feeling we had that you have to be better than others. Because they do not expect you to be good. So you don't have to be just good but better than everybody else. So whether it's a job interview or even if you have joined NCC, you can't just be a cadet, you have to be something. So the idea was to be into co-curricular activities, though none of us was really into sports. Generally, we were people who were doing things in schools and colleges.

So I think that was because…I won't say it was drilled into us but it was there in the air in our home that people expect you to be, you know, in our growing-up years generally Muslim students used to be fasaddi [lagging behind] in academics and others. And also when it came to jobs, again it was an understanding: let's suppose there is a bias, how do you overcome that bias? Not through push and pull, not somebody putting in a word for you, nobody will do that for you. For that you have to be good at what you do. So don't give the world a chance to kind of…walk over you or sideline you.

NE: So as a result you grew up thinking that it will be easier to sideline you because of your identity?

RJ: No, no. In fact, we had no sense of victimhood. No, I don't think any of us have a sense of it. My brother who is in the teaching profession, who now teaches in Delhi University, he had many frustrating years as the BJP was very strong with the ABVP lobby in Delhi University, where they had their own candidates. They did not want Muslims filling in their jobs. He went through a very long, frustrating time. Then it was very clear that he was not getting those teaching positions as he was not part of that clique. And the clique happened to be a very BJP clique. So that is something we knew.

But it was not something over which we beat our chest. He did eventually get the opportunity, and is teaching in Delhi University. Somebody came along who rose above that clique. We treated that more as an occupational hazard, rather than of us being singled out.

While indeed, he had been singled out. But there was no proof or anything. As this was not something that was written by someone somewhere. It's just a sense you have. The idea was to get over it. To somehow be better than others, you know.

NE: I guess every Muslim family has a similar sense of things in the work space to recount at some level. But that sense which you felt when you were younger, that stays with you, not so much in words. But subconsciously, how does it manifest itself?

RJ: But that empowers you, doesn't it? And I am very convinced of this. I don't think that it tells you to lie low or feel bad about yourself or sorry for yourself. No! It kind of empowers you to do more. Despite whatever people might think of you. It's there.

NE: With your belief or sense to excel in whatever you do, how have you handed that to your children?

RJ: They have to be good. Even if you are a cobbler.

NE: Does it have anything to do with your being Muslims?

RJ: Yeah...it has...in a way because people expect you to behave in a certain way because you are Muslim. But we bust that stereotype all the time, you know.

NE: With that busting thing, does it increase the pressure/burden on you?

RJ: No, it does not. I don't feel any burden on me at all. I see it as a great sense of liberation. Rather than a burden, I feel liberated by it. You know, today I am fifty-three years old and it gives me a good feeling.

NE: A sense of purpose, you mean to say?

RJ: No, a sense of good feeling. Maybe by nature I am non-conformist, which has nothing to do with Islam. I like to go against the grain. For me, possibly, it's just that. But it feels very good. I refuse to behave in the way I am expected.

Interview 17

With Dr Farrukh Waris, retired principal, Burhani College of Arts and Commerce, Mumbai

FW: Kids today have very heavy baggage to deal with, and part of that baggage they are bringing to their school. And let's agree that most families, be they Hindu or Muslim, they do talk about religion at home. But not in a way that includes others.

NE: As in?

FW: I consider myself a devout Muslim but very, very pragmatic and secular. Being secular is not a clichéd concept for us. My seven-year-old son was tutored by a maulana who taught him that *Mussulman bahut achhe hote hain, sabse mohabbat karte hain, aur kisi ke saath jhagda nahin karte* [Muslims are very good, they love everyone and they don't fight with anyone]. So all these beautiful values were etched in his mind. One day I find him telling a friend of ours, '*Moti uncle, hamare class mein sab Mussulman hain sirf Abraar aur Irfan nahin hai. Koi jhagda nahin karta lekin Irfan aur Abraar bahut jhagda karte hain.* [Moti uncle, everyone in our class is Muslim except Irfan and Abraar. Nobody fights with others, only Irfan and Abraar get into many fights.]' In his mind anyone who is non-aggressive is Muslim.

NE: Why should it be any different!

FW: Yes, another time my son came to me and said, '*Apurva toh Bhagwan kehta hai aur doosra friend Ishwar kehta hai, aap Allah miyan kehti hain.* [Apurva says Bhagwan, another friend calls god Ishwar and you say Allah miyan.] All the time, Allah miyan, Allah miyan... You ask me to pray to Allah miyan too...why?' So I say that when you love someone a lot then you refer to that person with so many names. Like your name is Sadayaan but I call you Saddu, or Saadu, or Chhotu. I have given you so many names. Similarly, with god we use so many names. If at that point I had said anything else, that would have been the benchmark in his mind to differentiate. I think in today's time of instant noodle news and views, we are missing out on handling such situations with the delicateness they need. All my three kids were brought up knowing about their religion but without any regimentation...in an open, informal way. They had the choice of doing namaz once, five times or never...that became their choice on growing up. Like the maths tutor came, the Hindi tutor came, music teacher, Kathak tutor, jazz [tutor], ballet tutor; similarly, the maulana came and did his bit. Although the maulana's intellect was never ever judged. There were no standards set. But knowing Persian and Urdu well, I would get upset when the maulana's *talaffuz* [pronunciation] wasn't good. I was OK with them giving basic education of the Quran. When my parents gave me religion they said, '*Jab hum doctor ke paas jaate hain toh doctor kehte hain, lal goli khana bukhaar utar jayega; peeli goli khana khansi chali jayegi.* [When we go to the doctor, he says, take the red pill and the fever will leave you; take the yellow pill to get rid of your cough.]' Similarly, my parents told me about the five pillars of Islam and if I stick to them then I am sorted for life. We just need to build their intelligence to understand human rights, have value systems and let them sort it out on their own.

Appendix 3

What can we do in schools?

Muslim Student in UP's Kanpur District Attempts Suicide after Teachers Call Him a Terrorist

Just as we were closing the edits for this book, I chanced upon above headline in various online news media platforms towards the end of September 2017. It was a story from Kanpur reported by the Indian news agency ANI. The story went like this: A class 11 student of Delhi Public School, Kalyanpur, in Kanpur district of Uttar Pradesh, attempted suicide after being repeatedly humiliated by schoolteachers and the principal, who had branded him a 'terrorist'. The boy is Muslim. On the night of 23 September, the student was admitted in a critical condition at a local hospital after attempting suicide by consuming sleeping pills and phenyl at his Swaroop Nagar residence.[1]

In a note he wrote before attempting suicide, the student spoke about the discrimination he experienced from his schoolteachers. 'Had joined school two months back. No one talked to me because the teachers asked them not to. Teachers and students targeted and taunted at me,' the student later told ANI.[2] On regaining consciousness at the hospital, he appealed to the chief minister, Yogi Adityanath, 'Chief minister sir, I am not a terrorist but a student.'

Though he was an ordinary middle-class student, his teachers viewed him with suspicion as if he was a terrorist. 'My bag is searched every day. I am made to sit in the last row in my class. If I ask anything, the teacher expels me from the class. Because of such conduct of the teachers, the other

---

[1] https://thewire.in/182453/suicide-attempt-student-up-discrimination/

[2] http://www.asianage.com/india/all-india/240917/kanpur-dps-student-attempts-suicide-after-harassment-by-4-teachers.html

students also maintain a distance from me,' he said.

Since the incident, the mother too suffered an anxiety attack and the family has shifted from Kanpur. While this case was an extreme example of where things are leading, it cannot be dismissed and should be a warning sign to all.

So what can a parent or a school do to counter communal bullying? Here are some suggestions:

1. Name it and address it: Do not gloss over issues or pretend they are not there. Teaching needs to catch up with the reality outside.
2. Choose to support: What you may feel is unnecessary to discuss might be urgent for some children and families. Many families are scared for their lives and safety. If you ignore that to focus on maths, that is problematic. We all experience the same events in different ways. Hatred is not necessarily experienced or perceived as hatred by all. It may be experienced as self-righteous indignation, justified anger or appropriate retaliation.
3. Be positive: Use positive examples that will help children see themselves reflected

positively. In an age when negative examples are in abundance, can each one of us embrace the positive?

4. Be calm: When a child reports an incident of bullying, be calm as you hear the child out. Children pick up messages from our tone much more than from our words. Teachers need to receive resources about how to talk about terror attacks and help children process what they are hearing. Teachers also need to ensure that children mix with each other.
5. Create 'diversity leaders': Form a point of contact/mentor in school for such incidents to be reported to. Someone easy and comfortable for the kids to talk and reach out to. Encourage reporting. Discourage pushing under the carpet. Administrations find few reports of anti-Muslim bias or harassment in their files. But the lack of data isn't due to a lack of bullying – Muslim kids aren't reporting the abuse. Students need to feel safe bringing up questions about religion and extremism. They have to be able to express their own misconceptions without being labelled.

6. Have open days for interfaith interactions: Invite a representative authority from all religions; let the children experience love of god from all faiths. Exposure can take the form of guest speakers, interfaith panels and a growing number of quality multimedia resources. This will also help address queries that some teachers might have pertaining to certain religions.

   Fostering interfaith understanding should be very much part of our collective nationalistic goals.
7. Actively check faith-coding: Surprised at a Muslim kid taking up Sanskrit instead of Urdu? Asking a Muslim kid to speak on Eid? You are not 'including' the Muslim kid by asking him/her exclusively to speak on their faith. Let the teacher get experts from outside or put together material. Don't let the student suffer because of your own laziness to reach out. Be more sensitive.
8. Check gendered Islamophobia: How are we helping the girls battle the stereotypes associated with them? Islamophobia gets

uglier when it is accompanied by gendered aggressive behaviour that goes further down the unreported data line.

9. Diversity in the teacher pool: Many of the real bullying examples we have are not from children but from teachers when they say things like 'You will become Osama bin Laden' or 'Modi taught people a lesson'. What are we doing to ensure that the teacher is not Islamophobic?
10. Be clear of your school's zero-tolerance policies: Almost all educators came to the profession with the aspiration to make a difference in the world. We are in a very challenging time as a society. This is a chance for our schools to foster the type of democratic ideals we want our children to aspire towards. Ultimately, when we help our students feel safe and included, they will be able to rise to their highest potential. Our work in classrooms and schools will also shape the leaders who will rise and hopefully become beacons of light for our society.

A Note on the Author

Nazia Erum has worked for the Global Fund and United Nations. She now runs a fashion start-up in Delhi-NCR.

AN EXTENSIVE LIBRARY

Including fresh, new, original Juggernaut books from the likes of Sunny Leone, Praveen Swami, Husain Haqqani, Umera Ahmed, Rujuta Diwekar and lots more. Plus, books from partner publishers and loads of free classics. Whichever genre you like, there's a book waiting for you.

juggernaut.in

DON'T JUST READ; INTERACT

We're changing the reading experience from passive to active.

Ask authors questions

Get all your answers from the horse's mouth. Juggernaut authors actually reply to every question they can.

Rate and review

Let everyone know of your favourite reads or critique the finer points of a book – you will be heard in a community of like-minded readers.

Gift books to friends

For a book-lover, there's no nicer gift than a book personally picked. You can even do it anonymously if you like.

Enjoy new book formats

Discover serials released in parts over time, picture books including comics, and story-bundles at discounted rates. And coming soon, audiobooks.

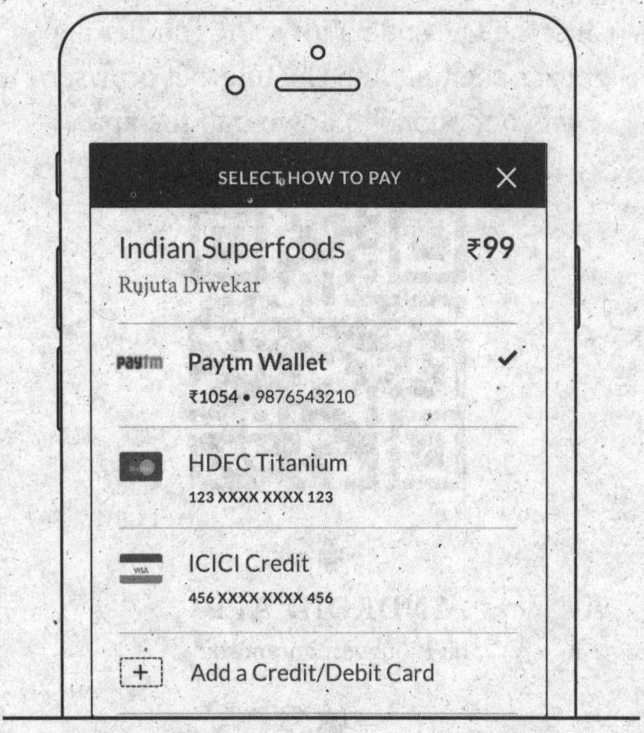

Paytm Wallet, Cards & Apple Payments

On Android, just add a Paytm Wallet once and buy any book with one tap. On iOS, pay with one tap with your iTunes-linked debit/credit card.

Click the QR Code with a QR scanner app or type the link into the Internet browser on your phone to download the app.

ANDROID APP

bit.ly/juggernautandroid

iOS APP

bit.ly/juggernautios

For our complete catalogue, visit www.juggernaut.in
To submit your book, send a synopsis and two sample chapters to books@juggernaut.in
For all other queries, write to contact@juggernaut.in